PRAISE FOR THE BOOKS OF
#1 INTERNATIONAL BESTSELLING AUTHOR
KERK MURRAY

Since the Day We Left

"Best romance I've read this year!"
— Reader Review

"Haven't cried that hard over a book in a long time."
— Reader Review

"I read this in one sitting on a rainy weekend and it was PERFECT. Already ordered copies for my book club."
— Reader Review

"Hadley Cove feels so real to me."
— Reader Review

"I picked up this book on a whim and now I'm ordering everything Kerk Murray has ever written."

— Reader Review

"I've been following Kerk Murray for years and his writing just keeps getting better. *Since the Day We Left* is on another level entirely."

— Reader Review

Since the Day We Wished

"I read it in one sitting! If you love small town romance with realistic characters, you need to read this. I already pre-ordered the next one."

— Reader Review

"Loved every page. The Wishing Tree concept was so romantic and unique. Kerk Murray is an auto-buy author for me now."

— Reader Review

"I hope this gets made into a movie. So good!"

— Reader Review

Since the Day We Kissed

"This is the first romance I've read written by a male and won't be my last by this author. His take on romance was surprisingly insightful—you can't help but cheer for Kara and Ethan."

— Reader Review

"The best story in the series by far!"

— Reader Review

"I can't wait to read more Kerk Murray books! He's my favorite new-to-me author."

— Reader Review

"I absolutely adore Hadley Cove! It felt like I was returning to my hometown."

Since the Day We Fell

— Reader Review

"I've been a fan of Kerk's work since *Pawprints On Our Hearts*, and *Since the Day We Fell* did not disappoint."

— Reader Review

Since the Day We Danced

"Murray's writing is simply gorgeous."

— The Book Commentary

"An emotional rollercoaster that will make you fall in love with love all over again."

— Reader Review

"A beautiful escapist Nicholas Sparks type romance."

— Reader Review

Pawprints On Our Hearts

"Animal lovers will feel connected to Murray's almost spiritual awakening and admire his devotion to following his heart, even in the face of tremendous sacrifice. This touching memoir overflows with intense emotion."

— Booklife by Publishers Weekly

"A deeply moving memoir... one of the best books that capture the connection between human beings and dogs... *Pawprints on Our Hearts* inspires a love for animals while exploring the painful edges of the human heart in need of love and healing."

— The Book Commentary

"A powerful and emotional story."

— Alyson Sheldrake, Bestselling author of "Kat the Dog"

BY KERK MURRAY

Since the Day We Left

KERK MURRAY

Since the Day We Left

Hadley Cove Sweet Romance: Book 5

Magnolia Press
Birmingham

Magnolia Press
105 Vulcan Rd
Ste 221
Birmingham, AL 35209

Library of Congress Cataloging-in-Publication Data

Names: Murray, Kerk, author.
Title: Since the Day We Wished/ Kerk Murray.
Description: First edition. | Birmingham: Magnolia Press, 2025.
Identifiers: LCCN 2025906280 | ISBN 9798992553819 (paperback) | ISBN 9798992553826 (hardcover)

Printed in the United States of America

For those who believe in magic,
and to the brave souls who start over
when all seems lost—this one's for you.

Before You Begin...

You're invited to join my private Facebook Reader Group, where you'll make new book friends, meet other animal lovers, and be the first to know about new releases, book clubs, and special deals.

Join today:
Kerk Murray's private Facebook Reader Group

facebook.com/groups/779562103953550

Story Playlist

Listen on your favorite music streaming platform.

kerkmurray.com/products/sincethedayweleftplaylist

Wendi's Listens

1. "Torn" — Natalie Imbruglia

2. "Beautiful" — Christina Aguilera

3. "I Wanna Dance with Somebody" — Whitney Houston

4. "Save the Best for Last" — Vanessa Williams

5. "Sparks Fly" — Taylor Swift

6. "This Is Why We Can't Have Nice Things" — Taylor Swift

7. "Head Above Water" — Avril Lavigne

8. "Everywhere" — Michelle Branch

9. "Drops of Jupiter" — Train

10. "Breathless" — The Corrs

Miles's Listens

1. "Kryptonite" — 3 Doors Down

2. "Here Without You" — 3 Doors Down

3. "Dare You to Move" — Switchfoot

4. "The Reason" — Hoobastank

5. "Gravity" — John Mayer

6. "Slide" — Goo Goo Dolls

7. "How You Remind Me" — Nickelback

8. "Home" — Daughtry

9. "Chasing Cars" — Snow Patrol

10. "Make You Feel My Love" — Adele

Welcome back to Hadley Cove!

This story began with two questions: What if a small act of kindness rippled decades into the future? What if two strangers, connected by a childhood encounter, found their way back to each other when they needed it most?

As you walk alongside Wendi and Miles, I hope you feel the weight of dreams deferred, the courage to rebuild after loss, and the beauty of life's unexpected encounters. Arthur's journey was written to honor the complex reality so many families face—the heartbreak of loss, but also the moments of clarity that remind us of who our loved ones have always been.

The Painted Shell is more than just a store; it's a crossroads—the choice between security and passion, between expectation and what truly makes us come alive. Through Wendi's struggle, I hope you find echoes of your own moments of bravery.

Thank you for being a part of this incredible adventure and for joining me in creating a more compassionate world for all living beings, one heartwarming story at a time.

Your support through reading and sharing this series, along with your kind words in messages and reviews, means more than I can express. I'm forever grateful.

Don't forget to check out the extras I've included at the
front and end of the book, created with you in mind.

♡ Kerk

"The shell, the beach, the quiet light;
All safe, all sure, all right."

—Sylvia Plath, *Full Fathom Five*

Prologue

Thirty-Six Years Earlier

A GLASS VASE SHATTERED against the wall, exploding into jagged shards.

Wilting wildflowers bobbed in the spreading puddle.

"This ain't working, June! Your part-time job ain't paying the bills!"

"Oh, so it's my fault now? You're the one who—"

"I don't wanna hear it! We need money, not excuses!"

Her dad stormed down the hall, leaving her mother in the middle of the living room, hands trembling at her side. When she turned to Wendi, her eyes were glassy with unshed tears. "Go play outside for a while, sweetheart. I just … I need to rest."

Rest meant crying. Wendi knew that by now.

She nodded, grabbed her sketchbook, and slipped out the back door, the screen clattering shut behind her.

The wind tangled Wendi's hair as she nestled into her favorite spot on the beach. At nine, her little alcove, hidden between weathered rocks and scraggly dune grass, felt like it belonged only to her.

She had stumbled upon it last summer, fleeing from girls who had made fun of her clothes. And now, this was where she always came when her parents' fights got too loud for the thin walls of their house.

A fiddler crab darted sideways, vanishing into the sand. Wendi smiled—even the tiniest creatures had their own places to hide.

Waves lapped at the shore while seagulls wheeled overhead. A feather drifted down, landing near her foot. Wendi picked it up, tucking it into the spiral binding of her sketchbook.

"The world is full of hidden treasures," her mom had told her once, during a rare beach day, gathering seashells. "If you're willing to look."

Wendi spotted a familiar lump in the sand. Reaching over, she brushed away the top layer and unearthed the small metal tin she'd buried a few days before. After shaking off the remaining grains, she pried open the lid and tipped the tin, letting her treasures tumble into her palm: a piece of sea glass the exact blue-green of her mother's eyes when she was happy; a perfect sand dollar; a shark tooth; and her prized possession—a spiral shell with bands of cream and caramel. She'd found it after a storm, half-buried, waiting just for her.

For a moment, she cradled them, then set them next to her. She pushed strands of hair away from her face as she focused on sketching the waves. Motion was the hardest thing to capture—waves never rested, just like her thoughts.

She paused, tilting her head, before shading in the foam where it touched the sand. Mrs. Abernathy had called her drawings a "genuine gift" last week.

She shifted on the sand, erasing a small smudge.

Dad didn't even look at my last art project.

A familiar knot formed in her throat, one she'd learned to swallow down while keeping the tears at bay. Her grip tightened on the pencil as she looked out toward the water.

"Not now, Wendi," he'd snapped, barely noticing the watercolor of a lighthouse she'd held out. "Can't you see I'm busy? Go show your mother."

She'd left without another word, tucking the painting into her folder. It remained unseen.

Wendi let out a slow breath, pushing the memory aside. She turned back to her sketchbook, tracing the faint horizon line where the sky and sea blurred together.

A shadow moved along the shoreline, and her pencil hovered mid-stroke.

No one ever came here. This place was *hers*.

But now, a man and a boy trudged along the shore. The man wore a dark suit, his tie flapping in the wind, and shoes dangling from one hand. The boy—her age, maybe a little older—had his hands shoved into his pockets. His dress pants were rolled at the ankles.

Something about them made Wendi's chest tighten.

Maybe it was their slow, careful steps, or the way they seemed disconnected from the beauty around them. They reminded her of the somber faces, the organ music, and the flowery scents at her grandma's funeral last year.

They stopped.

The boy flinched as the waves lapped his toes. The man placed a hand on the boy's shoulder.

Wendi shrank back into the safety of her hiding spot.

Reaching into his suit pocket, the man pulled out a small container and twisted the lid. He stepped into the surf and emptied it. Gray ash spilled out, swirling in the breeze. Some seemed to have clung to his fingers, which he rinsed before returning to the boy.

Wendi's chest tightened.

Someone's gone.

Forever.

The man tried to put his arm around the boy, but he jerked away, his face crumpling as tears streaked his cheeks.

The man looked helpless—the way adults sometimes did when they ran out of words. He glanced at the boy, then stepped deeper into the waves, his back to the shore, shoulders shaking. The water was up to his knees now.

The boy stood alone, his fist pressed to his mouth, stifling sobs. His other arm clutched his middle, as if holding himself together.

A hollow ache echoed inside Wendi. She knew what it was like to cry alone.

Her mom had always warned her about strangers: "Not everyone is nice just because they look like it."

But leaving the boy to cry alone felt wrong—like walking

past an injured bird and pretending not to see. So Wendi slid the spiral shell into her pocket and stood.

The boy didn't notice her until she was beside him. He startled, quickly wiping his face with his sleeve.

Wendi froze.

Does he even want me here? Maybe I should go.

For a beat, she waited quietly, giving him a chance to decide.

When he didn't move, she reached into her pocket and pulled out her spiral shell. She held it out, palm open. The sunlight caught the shell's swirls, making them glow.

"It's magic," she said. "From the ocean. It'll help."

On her worst days, she would hold it to her ear, listening to the ocean trapped inside. Its steady whooshing reminded her that some things stayed the same, no matter how much the world around her changed.

His deep brown eyes, swollen and red-rimmed, flicked between the shell and Wendi before he finally reached for it.

Their fingers brushed as he took the shell, sending a strange flutter through Wendi's stomach. He curled his fingers around it, gripping it tightly.

"Here," Wendi said, gently guiding his hand. "Hold it up to your ear, like this." She mimicked the motion with her empty hand.

His eyes drifted shut as he listened.

"Can you hear it?" She leaned forward, hopeful. "The ocean?"

The boy went still. Then, after a pause, he nodded—just barely. A look of wonder crept across his face—the same look she'd imagined she had worn when she'd first discovered the shell's magic. His eyes widened slightly, but he didn't say a word.

He didn't have to.

His breathing steadied, and his shoulders relaxed. The shell fit in his palm like it had been waiting for him, as it had once waited for her.

In that moment, Wendi understood—giving something away didn't leave behind an emptiness, but a quiet fullness, knowing it was exactly where it belonged.

She lowered herself onto the sand and hugged her knees to her chest. The boy hesitated, then sat too—still leaving space between them. He kept the shell clenched in his hand as they both watched the man in the waves.

Neither spoke.

The sun began its descent, turning the water into sheets of copper and rose gold, while shadows stretched across the sand.

Wendi knew it was time to go.

If she stayed out too late, her mom would worry, and the last thing she wanted was to add more sadness to the day. Standing up, she brushed the sand from her shorts and took a few steps backward. The boy looked up, still seated, still holding the shell.

When she turned to leave, Wendi couldn't help but glance over her shoulder one last time. The man had returned from the water and now stood beside the boy, who was holding up the shell, his lips moving—speaking. The man's gaze lifted, meeting Wendi's across the beach. He gave a small nod that she returned before continuing on her way.

Arriving back at her secret spot, where her sketchbook lay open beside the tin, she kneeled and reached for the scattered treasures, carefully placing them back inside. Then she snapped the lid shut, scooped out a shallow hole, and buried the tin, smoothing the sand before crossing a few twigs over it.

Wendi turned back to her sketchbook, dusting away the specks of sand. After a final glance at her work, she shut the book, secured the elastic band around the cover, and tucked it under her arm before heading home.

As she climbed the wooden steps leading away from the beach, something made her pause. Looking back, she saw the man and boy standing together, their heads bent over the tiny treasure she had given away.

Somehow, with one less piece, her collection felt more whole.

Her mom was right. The world *was* full of hidden treasures.

1

Wendi

Present Day

Sunday

AT THE FOOT OF the bed, a little Yorkipoo body unfurled in a sleepy stretch. A soft whine came, then another, more insistent. Max's paw nudged Wendi's shoulder.

She pulled the quilt tighter around her. The morning light filtered through the sheer linen curtains, and outside, the waves crashed against the shore.

"I'm up, I'm up," she groaned.

Her phone lit up, reading 6:47 a.m.—thirteen minutes before her alarm was set to go off. Max always managed to wake her right before. His black hair stood up in wild tufts, and his eyes were bright, ready for the day.

She swung her legs over the side of the bed and moved toward the door. Max jumped down to follow her.

"Morning, troublemaker."

She caught her reflection in the dresser mirror—hair twisted into gravity-defying angles and pillow lines etched across her face. Her former Manhattan-self would've gasped and reached for the straightener. Back then, mornings started at 4:30 a.m., with a calorie-tracked smoothie and an outfit chosen days in advance. Now, her routine consisted of staying in pajamas until she absolutely had to change, occasionally forgetting what day it was.

The beachfront cottage felt like a dollhouse compared to her Manhattan apartment, but what it lacked in size, it more than made up for in charm. Salt-worn siding, faded blue paint peeling in places. Mismatched furniture. Windows that sometimes stuck but framed perfect ocean views. Even the shower demanded a specific sequence of handle-turning that had taken weeks to master. But it was hers.

In the kitchen, she filled Max's bowl while the coffeemaker gurgled to life. She leaned against the counter, watching him devour his food with a single-minded focus.

It was hard to believe this was the same dog she'd rescued two years ago—the one who'd spent his first two days cowering under her bed. Back then, he'd been nothing but protruding ribs and skittish eyes.

"You've come a long way, sweet boy."

And so had she.

The woman who had once sobbed through a presentation to hotel executives, who had locked herself in a bathroom stall, hands shaking too much to even text James about what had happened, felt like a stranger now.

Not that he would've understood anyway.

"It's just nerves," he'd say. "Buckle down and push through."

She grabbed her mug—the one Emma had gifted her—with "Home is where your art is" painted in wobbly letters. The coffee warmed her hands as she slipped on sandals for their morning walk.

Outside, salt air filled her lungs as Max tugged at his leash, eager to reach the sand. The beach was nearly deserted—just a few joggers in neon running gear and the Hendersons, an elderly couple who had been married for fifty-seven years, walking arm-in-arm wearing matching windbreakers.

Max bounded toward the waves, kicking up bursts of sand before looping back, his eyes on her as if to say, "Did you see that?"

During those dark months after her breakdown—when she couldn't sleep, create, or even remember why she'd once loved her PR job—Max had been her constant. The reason she got out of bed.

"Ready to check out the shop, boy?" His ears perked up at the sound of the familiar phrase.

⁓ℯℓℯ⁓

The morning sun created a patchwork of gold and blue that changed with each drifting cloud as they headed toward Main Street, passing familiar landmarks—Mrs. Winters watering geraniums outside the candle shop, Old Pete setting up his newspaper stand, the scent of fresh coffee floating from Phil's Diner. These were the details she once would've missed back in the city, too busy sipping her venti latte and scrolling through emails on her phone.

"Morning, Pete."

"Another beautiful November day, Wendi-girl," he called back. "Good weather for selling some art supplies, huh?"

She stretched her lips into what she hoped passed for optimism. The week before, she'd gone a whole four days without a single customer.

Walking on, she couldn't help but notice how Hadley Cove had changed since her childhood. A high-end seafood restaurant had replaced the antique shop where she'd gotten her first job. The old record store where she'd spent hours browsing vinyl records with friends had been replaced by a boutique selling overpriced beach decor to tourists. And the old barn, where she'd had her first kiss, had been converted into an event venue for weddings and retreats.

Some changes hurt more than others though—like driving past her parents' empty house on Sycamore Street, sold after her mother's funeral five years ago. The shutters, once a cheerful yellow, were now a dull beige. The oak tree in the front yard—the one she used to climb while her dad pretended not to see—stood untouched. But the porch swing was gone, and the flower beds her mother had once tended to were nothing but weeds now, creeping toward the cracked walkway. When her mother had passed, she'd come back only for the funeral—a twelve-hour visit, a handful of obligatory condolences, and then straight to the airport. And for her father's funeral three years before that? She hadn't come at all.

She told herself he wouldn't have expected her to. That he understood why she'd stayed away.But sometimes, late at night, she wasn't so sure.

Still, the heart of the town—the soul—remained. The boardwalk was lined with vendors selling saltwater taffy and trinkets. In the nearby park, the old Wishing Tree stood as tall as ever, its branches filled with faded ribbons tied by generations of hopeful souls. From the town square, the clock still chimed on the hour—except between 6:00 p.m. and 6:00 a.m. And through it all, Old Pete remembered exactly how she liked her ice cream—strawberry with rainbow sprinkles.

Hadley Cove had always been the place she'd left and never the place she returned to. That teenage Wendi Parker had sworn she'd never move back to. But when everything in Manhattan had crumbled—her marriage, her career, her sense of self—where else was there to go? Thirty-seven years of running had brought her straight back here. She knew better than anyone that sometimes, the places we ran from were the ones that knew us best.

Two teenagers zipped past on skateboards, calling out to someone across the street. Their carefree energy reminded her of summers with her childhood friend, Emma, racing bikes down these same streets, hair flying behind them, making plans for futures that seemed impossibly distant and perfectly certain at the same time.

Just ahead, The Painted Shell sat on the corner of Maple

and Main, its blue exterior standing out against the surrounding buildings. Wendi had painted the sign herself—a spiral shell with swirls of color emerging from its center. Max waited patiently as she unlocked the door, the brass bell chiming softly.

She flipped on the lights, illuminating her creation. Art supplies lined the walls—watercolors, acrylics, brushes, canvases, and specialty papers. A small gallery area displayed local artists' work, including a few of her own. The teaching space in the back held four tables for classes.

The shop had been a bakery, and a lingering scent of yeast and sugar was still detectable on humid days. She'd chosen it for the large windows that flooded the space with natural light and the wooden floors—it was also all she could afford.

Next week's calendar hung by the register. More empty squares than filled ones. Tuesday's beginner class had one name penciled in. Wednesday—the art auction fundraiser … Her eyes paused on it.

Future Wendi will handle that. Hopefully.

And her pride and joy: Friday's "Art Therapy" session for the local community center. The last class never made money. She offered it for free to whoever needed it—but more often than not, she found herself rearranging chairs in the empty room. But when the class filled, even if just for a few hours, it felt like a small victory.

Every corner reflected her touch, from the hand-painted color wheel and shelves she'd stained herself, to the way she arranged drawing pencils by hardness rather than brand, from 9B to 9H.

This was hers—created from nothing but a dream and a divorce settlement.

For better *or* worse, right?

Max settled into his plush bed by the window as Wendi opened the ledger. The numbers stared back with brutal honesty.

Another month of scraping by.

She closed the book with a decisive snap, refusing to spiral so early in the morning. Instead, she arranged a display of sketchbooks.

But the numbers haunted her anyway.

- Rent: $1,500.

- Utilities: $320.

- Insurance: $440.

Her personal expenses had been whittled down to almost nothing—no cable, no streaming services, and groceries purchased strategically around sales and soon-to-expire markdowns.

Last month, she'd cleared $1,773 in sales. The month before: $2,105.

The credit card she'd sworn never to use for business expenses now carried a $6,200 balance, while her savings account had dwindled to $11,437—enough for perhaps five more months at this rate.

Back in her old life, she'd earned enough to never check price tags, to hail cabs without calculating the cost, and to order takeout without a second thought. Six figures plus bonuses, direct deposited and largely unappreciated while she'd been too busy to spend it. The irony wasn't lost on her—having money when she was too miserable to enjoy it, and now finding joy in work that couldn't sustain her. At forty-five, she should've been well on her way to retirement planning, not starting over.

The shrill ring of her phone cut through her ruminations. Laurel's name flashed on the screen—her former boss at Pinnacle Hotels.

Wendi's finger hovered over the green button. She could've let it go to voicemail. But ...

"Laurel, hi." She kept her voice even.

"Wendi! Finally, I get to hear that voice again." Laurel's words came in rapid-fire, overlapped with Manhattan traffic. "How's that tiny beach town treating you?"

"It's good. Quiet. Just what I needed."

"So ... tell me you've gotten this art phase out of your system, because I've got an offer you won't want to pass up." The familiar intensity in Laurel's voice made Wendi's chest tighten.

"I'm listening."

"Singapore's back on the table, and I need someone who speaks their language—metaphorically speaking. I want you. Better hours than before. More work-life balance. Three days a week in the city and one weekend a month—you could keep your beach cottage. Starting salary will be twenty percent higher than when you left."

The amount made Wendi's knees buckle. She gripped the edge of the counter for support.

More than The Painted Shell would make in three years.

"You don't have to answer now," Laurel continued. "Take two weeks. The position opens on the fifteenth, but I'm holding it for you. The board specifically asked for you."

Wendi took a deep breath. "That's … generous."

"It's pragmatic. We've been through three people since you left—none of them had your instincts." A car horn blared in the background. "Take your time. Think it over. Call me when you're ready to rejoin civilization."

The call ended, leaving Wendi clutching her phone, heart racing and palms damp—the same creeping symptoms that had preceded her breakdown.

Laurel Sullivan was the woman who'd plucked her from the marketing department eight years ago after hearing her smooth over a catastrophe with an irate hotel client. "You have a gift for reshaping reality," Laurel had told her. "You don't just solve problems—you make people forget there was ever a problem at all."

It had felt like a compliment then. Four promotions and countless crises later, Wendi recognized it for what it was—Laurel's talent for identifying useful tools. That's what she'd been—a tool to deploy against bad press, disgruntled clients, and public relations nightmares.

Still, they'd made a formidable team. Wendi crafting narratives that transformed ordinary hotels into exclusive experiences, Laurel cutting through corporate politics to implement them. When a celebrity trashed a penthouse suite, Wendi had not only prevented negative press but had somehow spun it into a feature in Architectural Digest about the hotel's renovation program. When bedbugs had been discovered in the Chicago location, she'd managed to redirect focus to their new organic cleaning protocols, actually increasing bookings the following quarter.

She'd been good at it. Too good, perhaps. Good enough that even her spectacular meltdown hadn't completely burned her bridges.

Feeling her heart rate climbing, Wendi closed her eyes and pressed her fingertips together into a fragile steeple. She then pushed her palms against each other, focusing on the pressure points where they connected. With each point of contact, she mentally named a color in her studio—cadmium red, cerulean blue, burnt amber, titanium white—a grounding technique her therapist had taught her.

Dr. Abrams' voice echoed in her memory: "Anxiety tells us stories about a future that may never happen. Bring yourself back to what is real right now."

Real: the pressure of my palms, the colors surrounding me, Max's steady presence beside me.

She reached for the bottle of water she kept behind the counter, savoring the sensation of cool liquid against her throat, the weight of the bottle in her hand. Eighteen months ago, this same trigger would have sent her spiraling. Six months ago, she might have needed to call Dr. Abrams. Today, she could still feel the anxiety—uncomfortable, yes, but no longer terrifying. No longer defining her.

She'd come that far, at least.

The first time Dr. Abrams had demonstrated the finger-steepling technique, Wendi had almost walked out.

This is what I'm paying two hundred dollars an hour for? she'd thought, the woman who'd negotiated million-dollar contracts, who'd managed teams of professionals, and who'd juggled crisis calls on three continents.

But they worked.

Anxiety couldn't co-exist with full presence in the moment. At least not the debilitating kind that had once sent her to the emergency room, convinced she was having a heart attack.

Max nudged against her calf, his wet nose leaving a damp circle on her skin. She sank to her knees and buried her face in his soft curls. His heart thumped against her cheek.

"What do you think, boy?" She scratched his ears. "Take the job or stick it out here and survive on ramen until the bank comes knocking?"

2

Miles

"I FOUND HIM WANDERING the beach, Miles. In his pajamas. He was calling your mother's name. He didn't know how to get home."

Mrs. Winters' 2:00 a.m. call had sent him packing within the hour. No hesitation. No second-guessing. Just him, his truck, and a bag stuffed together in the dark.

Not that there was much to leave behind.

A rented room. Jobs that barely covered rent. And a couple of guys he drank with at Flanagan's every Thursday—none of them close enough to ask why he still woke up in the middle of the night, soaked in sweat.

Here we are.

Miles pulled into the driveway, squinting as the mid-morning sun bounced off the faded coral siding of his dad's beach house. He drained the last cold sip of gas station coffee and climbed out of his truck.

Ocean air hit him as his boots sank into the sandy driveway. Palm fronds and broken seashells crunched beneath each step.

The porch came into view—one corner occupied by a rocking chair with a fraying wicker seat, and an old Coleman cooler doubling as a side table in the other. His dad's DIY wind chimes—fishing line strung with seashells—fluttered from the porch roof, clinking softly in the breeze. The AC unit jutted from the bedroom window, a recent addition after Miles had nearly melted through the last Fourth of July.

As he approached the house, he noticed the mailbox leaning to one side, half-swallowed by knee-high grass. Strips of paint curled from steps, and a lone shutter dangled from a single hinge, swaying like it might give up at any moment.

"Good grief, Dad," he muttered, stooping to gather a stack of soggy newspapers slumped against the door.

He took a deep breath and knocked.

Once. Twice. Three times.

Then another.

Finally, the door swung open. His dad stood there in rumpled pajamas and a misaligned button-up shirt. Arthur's silver hair stuck out in all directions, and something—maybe oatmeal—had dried at the corner of his mouth. For a heartbeat, Arthur's gaze drifted past Miles, seeming to search the empty air before settling on him.

"Miles." Arthur's face brightened. "You're early. The drive from Atlanta must've been quick."

"Morning, Dad." He forced a smile. "Five hours instead of six. Empty roads will do that."

Miles stepped inside. The shirt that had once pulled across his dad's shoulders now hung loose and the cuffs dangled past his wrists.

"Your mom ran to the store." Arthur shuffled toward the kitchen. "She'll be back soon."

Miles's stomach knotted.

Thirty-six years gone, yet his dad spoke like she'd only just stepped out. Miles had been just ten when she'd passed. At forty-six, he'd now lived nearly four times as long without her as with her. He sometimes struggled to remember the sound of her voice.

"Could use some coffee," Miles said, setting his bag down. "Want a cup?"

"Already started." Arthur gestured toward an empty coffeepot with water stains tracking down its side before moving from cabinet to cabinet—opening one, then another, then circling back—while Miles stepped away and surveyed the living room.

Piles of unread mail. Dishes with crusty food remnants. A blanket in a heap on the floor, like his dad had been sleeping on the couch. Dust covered the framed photos—Miles's graduation, his parents' anniversary, and his mom in the hospital when he was born.

And then the paintings. Stacked. Propped. Covering every inch of available space.

Almost all showed the same scene: the cove where they'd spread his mom's ashes. Some at sunrise, others at sunset, the water shifting from silver to gold to dark blue. But the curve of the shore and the rocks remained constant. In each one, two small figures stood at the water's edge—a man and a boy.

CRASH!

Miles snapped back from his thoughts.

He bolted.

"Dadgummit!" Arthur shouted. He stood in the middle of the kitchen, his right hand clenched against his side. Coffee grounds lay like black sand across the counter, dripping down onto the floor. Fragments of glass glinted on the tile where the coffeepot had exploded.

"Dad—" Miles approached, stepping carefully around the glass shards.

Arthur flinched.

"I need to check it." Miles took his dad's hand, finding a red mark where hot water had scalded him. He led Arthur over to the sink. "It's not too bad," Miles said, running cool water over the burn. "Where's your first aid kit?"

"First aid ..."

"Medicine cabinet? Bathroom?"

Silence.

"Dad?"

Arthur looked up, blinking rapidly, his forehead creased. "Arthur, you need to finish that painting before the Lighthouse Festival. They're expecting five new pieces by Friday."

"Dad ..." Miles tried to swallow the lump in his throat. "It's me, Miles. Your son."

Arthur yanked his hand away, splashing water on the counter. "I know who you are. But we need to go. Before she leaves."

"Before who leaves?"

"Elaine!" Arthur's eyes cleared with sudden urgency. "Your mom. She's waiting for us at the cove." He patted his pockets. "Where's my keys?"

"Dad, I don't—"

"The painting I finished yesterday—where is it? I need to bring it to her."

"Which one?"

"The cove." Arthur's voice cracked. "The one with her in it. She gave it to me—I have to give it back."

The back of Miles's neck prickled. His dad wasn't just confused; he was somewhere else entirely.

Miles spotted a canvas propped against the fridge—another cove scene, this one at twilight, painted in deep purples and blues. He carefully stepped around the broken glass and picked it up. "This one?"

Arthur's hands trembled as he reached for it. "No. Not this one. The colors are all wrong." His fingers drifted over the painted shoreline. "The sun was setting, and ..."

Miles unclenched his fists, one finger at a time. The Alzheimer's pamphlets from Dr. Mendez's office flashed through his mind.

Redirect, don't correct.

Miles took a deliberate breath and softened his tone. "Tell me more, Dad."

As Arthur went on, his shoulders gradually relaxed and Miles guided him toward a kitchen chair. Once he was seated, Miles quickly swept up the glass.

His dad smiled. "It was perfect."

That smile—the same one from Little League games and high school graduation, the one that had somehow held steady at his mom's funeral—was still there, even as the rest of him slipped away.

Miles nodded and grabbed the kettle. "Let's have some tea instead."

While the kettle heated, Miles wiped coffee grounds from the counter, keeping one eye on his dad. The hardest part of loving someone, he realized, wasn't the sacrifice; it was watching them search for pieces of themselves they might never find again.

"I'm sorry," Arthur said after a long silence. "It's happening more often, isn't it?"

Miles paused. "We're figuring it out, Dad. One day at a time."

"Your mom was always better at this—knowing what to say." Arthur glanced at the painting. "She would've helped me remember."

The kettle whistled, and Miles busied himself with mugs and tea bags, grateful for the distraction from the sheen in his eyes. His dad—who had taught him to catch a football, to change a tire, to get back up after falling—now looked at him with such trust and uncertainty that, despite all the research he'd done and the professionals he'd talked to, Miles still felt completely unprepared.

"You're doing fine." He placed a mug of tea in front of his dad, along with a sketchpad and pencil from the table. "How about you show me how to draw the cove?"

Arthur picked up the pencil and, with sure strokes, he sketched the shoreline, the rocks, and the meeting of sky and sea.

While his dad worked away, Miles slipped onto the back

porch for a moment alone. The ocean stretched endlessly before him. He leaned against the railing, breathing in the salty air, trying to loosen the tightness in his chest.

He pulled out his phone and scrolled through the string of texts he'd sent within ten minutes of Mrs. Winters' call.

Sorry, Mrs. Hendricks. Family emergency. Can't mow this week.

Hey Jim, need to raincheck on fixing that deck. My dad needs me in Hadley Cove.

Megan, can you cover my dog walking route for a few days? Family stuff.

Just three texts and he was free. No plants to water. No pet to feed. No one waiting for him. Three years of drifting. Running. Remembering the fire climbing those walls—and how, for the first time in his life, he had frozen.

Miles let out a breath, shaking his head like he could clear it. The screen door creaked behind him.

"The light's better in the morning," Arthur said, stepping onto the porch with his sketchpad. "That's when I like to paint the cove. The way the sun hits the water, it's like seeing the world being born again."

Miles studied his dad's sketch—lines drawn by a man trying to hold on to what time had already erased. "It's good, Dad. Really good—the rocks, the shore, the dunes."

"Your mom loved this place." Arthur didn't look away from the horizon. "That's why I bought the house. To keep her close."

Miles swallowed, then nodded toward the door. "Come on, Dad. Let's eat."

Back inside, Miles pulled open the fridge. Wilted spinach.

The last two end pieces of wholegrain bread, left in an untied bag. A half-used lemon in the crisper had shriveled and hardened. The almond milk—still technically in date—smelled questionable. Digging through the pantry, he found a can of chickpeas pushed to the back.

Mental note: First thing tomorrow, groceries.

He drained and rinsed the chickpeas, then mashed them with a fork while heating a pan he found after opening three different cabinets. As the chickpeas sizzled, he tossed in the spinach and seasoned with the few spices he could find in his dad's pantry.

"Hope you still like chickpea scramble." Miles set down two mismatched plates—one cracked, the other too small.

Arthur watched as Miles sat down across from him. "I've painted the cove a thousand times," he said between bites. "Morning, evening, summer, winter. It's never the same, not really." He pointed toward the living room with his fork, dropping food onto his shirt without noticing. "That one store in town used to sell them. People like beach paintings."

"They're good, Dad. More than good." Miles meant it. Despite everything, his dad's talent remained intact.

"It's been a while since I went down there," Arthur said, brushing his sleeve across his mouth. "My knees aren't what they used to be."

"Maybe we could go together. When you feel up to it." Miles stacked their plates, noting the half-eaten meal. "Let me finish unpacking, and we'll figure out what to do today."

In the guest room—now his room—Miles scanned the walls and the twin bed. The walls were bare, save for a single watercolor print of a lighthouse. Dust coated the dresser, and the sheets smelled musty. A draft whistled beneath the gap in the window frame and through the curtains that had certainly lost their color years ago. The closet door hung open, revealing empty hangers and a single cardboard box. It wasn't much, but it would do.

His visits had always been brief—holidays wedged between excuses to rush back to Atlanta, to whatever job was paying the bills.

Miles unzipped his duffel. Three T-shirts, two pairs of jeans, socks, underwear. That was it. Everything else was still in his truck—if there even was more.

When had it become so easy to pack his life away?

At the bottom of his duffel, something wrapped in a handkerchief waited. He paused.

Slowly, he unwrapped the small wooden box, its lid carved with a sunflower—his mom's favorite keepsake box, and one of the few things recovered from the fire. His finger brushed over the scorch marks along one edge, a permanent reminder of that night.

The hinges creaked as he lifted the lid, revealing a velvet lining—once midnight blue—now a soft indigo. In the center lay the single object that had traveled with him to the fire station, touched before each shift and slipped into his pocket. The thing he'd clung to through sleepless nights. Pressed to his ear when his dad's diagnosis had come. Gripped tight through the evening his career had fallen apart.

His breath steadied.

He reached for it. It felt the same—solid, smooth, real.

Just like that day on the beach. The day they'd scattered his mother's ashes.

His thumb traced the ridges as he slowly turned the spiral shell.

Then—her voice. Small. Sure. Cut across the years:

"It's magic," the little girl with kind green eyes had told him. "From the ocean. It'll help."

3

Wendi

THE MORNING DRAGGED ON.

Three customers had wandered in, spent little, and left. A tourist picked up a lighthouse print. A high schooler tried (and failed) to haggle over paintbrushes. Mrs. Cooper, loyal as ever, bought paper for her grandson.

Total sales: Forty-seven dollars and sixteen cents—less than dinner for two at the bistro down the street.

Retirement by ninety-five?

Wendi turned to find Max on a cushion by the window, stretched out on his side. A patch of his hair caught the sunlight, and occasionally, his paws twitched as he dozed.

At least one of us is living the dream.

The shop phone hadn't rung once all day. Not even one of those scam calls offering an extended warranty on a car she no longer owned. Her inbox wasn't much better. No online orders, just a newsletter from the Chamber of Commerce recapping last week's town hall meeting she'd missed.

Today's inventory check had also been yet another exercise in denial. The high-quality watercolor paper—the expensive German kind professional artists favored—hadn't sold a single sheet in months. Next to them, the handmade brushes from the artisan in Birmingham had become permanent fixtures in their display. Even the student-grade acrylics were collecting dust.

By 2:30 p.m., Wendi was setting up for the watercolor workshop. Two students had signed up—better than last week's one, but still far from the twelve needed to turn a profit. She arranged brushes, filled water cups, and set out palettes like soldiers in formation. Then she reorganized the colored pencils one by one, ensuring each was perfectly parallel, even though no one had touched them in days. Back in New York, she'd had an entire team for this—visual merchandizing specialists who understood sightlines and customer behavior. Here, she only had instinct and hope, neither proving particularly effective for sales.

When the final pencil clicked into place, Wendi exhaled and stepped back. Hands on hips, she surveyed her handiwork. There was something soothing about it, the careful symmetry. The store might have been failing, but nobody would ever have guessed it from the way her displays looked.

Small wins.

The flyer on the door caught Wendi's attention, *Save The Shell* printed at the top in bold, hopeful letters. She stared at the date.

Three more days.

She'd spent yesterday sorting through potential auction

items—mostly her own pieces that hadn't sold and a few donations from former students. Nothing that would command the kind of money The Painted Shell needed to survive. The stack looked pathetically small against the back wall. Her gaze lifted to the mural above it—the one she'd started the week she opened. A year later, it was still unfinished, much like everything she hadn't gotten to.

This was it. Her last shot. If the auction failed, so did the shop.

She needed something big. Something to make people believe this place was worth saving.

The bell over the door jingled—a sound far more cheerful than Wendi felt—as Emma breezed in with a brown paper bag. A golden retriever trotted in beside her, tail wagging in a wide arc.

"Riley, careful," Emma said, guiding him away from the shelves. Riley immediately spotted Max and bounded over.

Max jumped off his cushion and circled the much larger dog with excited little yips. Riley gave a gentle woof and rubbed noses with his tiny friend.

"Special delivery for His Royal Highness, Sir Max-a-lot," Emma announced, swinging the bag. "Our new sweet potato and peanut butter treats—Riley-approved, four paws up."

Max momentarily abandoned his playdate and scampered to Emma's feet.

"You're turning him into a treat snob," Wendi said with a chuckle.

"We both know he deserves them for being the sweetest boy." Emma hopped onto the stool behind the counter. "Alright, out with it. What's the face about?"

"What face?"

"The 'I'm fine, except I'm definitely not' face." Emma's red hair flared like a struck match in the light as she leaned in. "Come on, we've been friends since we put worms in Joey Miller's lunch box. You can't hide from me."

Wendi tugged at a loose thread on her shirt. "Laurel called. Made me an offer."

Emma's smile faltered. "And?"

"And ... it's tempting. Better hours. More money. Three days in the city, one weekend a month, four days here. I could keep the cottage."

"But that means going back to corporate. Remember what that did to you? The panic attacks? That night you called me in tears after—"

"I remember. I also remember paying bills without checking my account balance first."

"Fair. Though I've noticed a suspicious lack of ramen in your pantry. Pantries don't lie."

"Still a ramen girl—for now. But last week, I put real vegetables in it. That's growth."

"Progress." Emma smirked, then squeezed her arm. "Whatever you decide, I'm in your corner. But that store?" She nodded toward Barking Orders across the street. "Took me ten years to make it real. First two years? Nothing but pasta. My paycheck? Might as well have been Monopoly money."

"Technically, ramen is pasta."

"You know what I mean. Good things take time." Emma glanced at her watch. "Oh shoot, I gotta go. Promised Luke and Jeremiah I'd grab lunch."

"Yeah, I should probably eat something too. Good seeing you." Wendi stepped closer to hug her friend.

Emma whistled for Riley, then held up a hand. "Wait—before I go, we *must* uphold the sacred handshake. As decreed in the *Officially Official Redhead Rulebook*, section three, paragraph two."

"Ah yes, the code must be honored. The code is law, after all," Wendi said, standing.

They launched into their ritual—three quick slaps, pinky hook, hip bump, and jazz hands finale—moving in perfect unison.

"Still flawless," Emma said.

"Truly, our finest middle school accomplishment."

Emma hugged her again. "Never forget—there's two kinds of people in this world: Team Ginger and the unfortunate rest. We, my friend, are the chosen ones."

⸳ℓℓ⸳

Emma's words stuck with her through the workshop. The two students, Mrs. Winters and Old Pete, seemed to enjoy creating seascapes. Wendi demonstrated how to layer paint to capture the transparency of waves while her thoughts ping-ponged between her life in Hadley Cove and Laurel's offer.

"Oh dear, I've made a mess of it." Mrs. Winters sighed, dabbing at a blob of white bleeding into her shoreline.

"That's not a mistake—it's an opportunity," Wendi said. "Some of the best art comes from accidents." She helped

Mrs. Winters incorporate the "mistake" into a deeper wave shadow.

"You make it look easy, Wendi-girl," Old Pete said, his hand hovering over his canvas.

Wendi smiled and adjusted the angle of his brush. "There. That should help."

At the end of class, Mrs. Winters held her painting at arm's length, beaming. "My granddaughter's birthday is next month. I think she might actually want this one." She carefully set it on the drying rack. "And I'll bring Susan next time. She's been looking for something to do since her husband passed."

Wendi nodded, watching them gather their things. She'd heard these promises before—well-intentioned, but often forgotten. Still, Mrs. Winters had improved over the three sessions she'd attended. That had to count for something, right?

Old Pete placed his painting on the drying rack, making sure it wouldn't touch the others. "Same time next week, Wendi-girl? Keeps these old hands from rusting up." He tipped an imaginary hat and gestured to his painting with a wink. "Might even frame that one for the hallway."

"Your spot's safe, Pete." A familiar warmth bloomed in Wendi's chest as he straightened his coat and shuffled toward the door. She still remembered him changing her flat tire in the rain when she was seventeen, soaked but refusing help, with a simple, "That's how we do things in this town, Wendi-girl."

These small connections—they didn't pay the bills, but they mattered in ways she couldn't quite articulate.

Amber light glowed along the path as Wendi and Max made their way to the secluded cove. The hidden spot required traversing a narrow path through dune grass and around rocks that discouraged tourists. Beyond the jagged rocks, the tide pools near the outcrop had been miniature universes to her younger self—ecosystems she'd study for countless hours, filling sketchbooks with drawings of waves, birds, starfish, and tiny crabs.

A breeze rolled in from the water, carrying the distinctive scent of low tide. Sea oats swayed, creating a rustling soundtrack that never failed to calm her. Plovers skittered along the wet sand, leaving tiny three-pronged tracks that disappeared with each wave.

"We're here, boy." Wendi kicked off her sandals, sinking her toes into the cool sand. Max explored nearby while she settled onto a flat rock. Opening her sketchbook, she began translating the ocean's movements into lines and shadows on the paper. Her thoughts shifted to the treasure tin she had buried decades before.

It was long gone—she'd looked for it when she moved back last year. She'd half-expected to find it still there. Though the childhood beach treasures were gone, the spot remained the same.

Her pencil paused mid-stroke. The boy in the funeral clothes flickered in her mind—standing at the shore, thirty-six years ago, while the man—his dad, she'd assumed—scattered ashes into the waves. Over the years, she'd wondered about him. She hoped he was okay wher-ever he was now. Sometimes she imagined him grown, per-haps with children of his own, maybe even telling them about the girl who'd given him a "magic" shell on the worst day of his life.

The sketch beneath her hands had taken shape—not just waves now, but the precise spot where the sky met water, that liminal space where elements merged.

Two weeks to decide.

Memories of her Manhattan life surfaced—floor-to-ceil-ing windows showcasing a sliver of Central Park, the door-man who'd always greeted her by name, the espresso ma-chine that had cost more than her first month's rent in Hadley Cove, the wardrobe of tailored suits in neutral tones, the reservations at restaurants with month-long waiting lists, and the contacts who could get her into any event.

Going back to Pinnacle meant security—a steady pay-check and health insurance that actually covered things. The salary Laurel offered would not only erase her cash flow problems, but she could also keep the cottage and The Painted Shell open, even if it was only part time. No more anxiety when the electric bill arrived. No more mental mu-sical chairs about which debt to tackle first. No more ramen dinners.

But it would mean returning to a world where colleagues had watched her hyperventilate during the brand relaunch, where her divorce from James had fueled months of gossip. Where her creativity had been limited to finding new ways to say "exclusive," "luxurious," and "world-class" with-out sounding repetitive, and spinning control for wealthy guests who thought their minor inconveniences were catastrophes.

Who had she been there? Just another face in the blur of a morning commute? Another overworked professional eating takeout alone at her desk? When had success started to feel so ... hollow?

Wendi stared out at the water. Here in Hadley Cove, she created art that spoke to her soul. She taught others to find their creative voice. She woke to the sound of waves instead of honking taxis. She had time to breathe, to heal.

It also meant the dwindling savings account despite her best efforts, credit card debt mounting each month, and the fear that another slow season would sink everything.

A year ago, the choice had been easy. Now? Not so much.

Wendi knew some decisions didn't come with a right answer. Just a choice, and the hope that you could live with it.

Security or passion? Structure or freedom? The devil she knew or the dream she'd been fighting for? Safety had never felt like freedom. And freedom had never felt safe.

She closed her sketchbook with a sigh, brushed sand from her capris, and stood. The last of the daylight had faded, and the first stars emerged, dotting a sky washed in violet and gold. In the distance, a boat's flickering lights cut through the darkening waters.

"Time to head home, boy."

Silence.

"Max?" She turned in a slow circle, scanning the beach—empty sand, endless ocean. A flutter of unease rippled through her chest. "Max!"

She hurried toward the dunes where she'd last seen him sniffing a clump of sea grass. Nothing.

Further up the beach? Empty.

Back toward the path? Not there either.

Her pulse hammered in her ears. Max never wandered far. He had to be close. She cupped her hands to her mouth. "Max, want a treat?"

The familiar phrase that always grabbed his attention had to work, right?

She listened, straining against the sound of waves. Nothing.

Scenarios flashed through her mind—Max swept out by a wave. Max falling into a crevice between rocks. Max taken or worse ...

"Max!" His name tore from her throat, sharper now.

Wendi fumbled for her phone, flicked on the flashlight, and swept it beneath the rock outcropping. Just sand.

She sprinted along the shoreline, calling his name, pausing between calls to listen for the faint jingle of his collar tags. "Please, Max! Where are you?"

No pattering of paws. No scampering black blur.

Nothing.

4

Miles

"Look at that," Arthur said, stopping in his tracks. He nodded toward the water, where moonlight bounced off the waves. "Would've been perfect to paint. Should've brought my gear."

Miles followed his gaze. "Yeah?"

"See how the moon's hitting the water there?" Arthur pointed, tracing the path with his finger. "A bit of white with navy—dark gray for the shadows. The trick's in the shine."

Earlier, his dad might've forgotten for a moment that Miles was his son, but he could still rattle off paint colors as if reading from a catalog.

They continued along the dry, cool sand as waves rolled in with a steady hush, and stars blinked overhead.

"Remember that lady who kept saying I used too much orange?" Arthur asked. "At the show in Buckhead?"

Miles nodded. "Mrs. Marcy. She still bought three of your

paintings."

"Should've charged her double."

"Too late now." Miles laughed. "We could come back tomorrow or next week and bring your supplies."

Arthur's face brightened. "Yes. Late morning would be perfect. The light'll be different." He turned slowly. "The tide'll be lower. Those rocks will make good foreground elements."

Miles made a mental note to check if they had enough canvases. He'd also need to dig out the travel easel—the one he'd bought for Arthur's sixtieth. They'd taken it on weekend trips to the mountains. Despite his dad's complaints about "lugging this garbage," he'd admitted, "it did the job."

A spark of unexpected comfort flickered inside Miles. *Maybe the beach is helping?*

Dr. Mendez had mentioned how environmental triggers sometimes helped ground patients in their memories.

"Remember how I used to bring you here?" Arthur asked, hand at waist level. "When you were about this high?"

Or maybe it isn't helping at all.

Dr. Mendez had also warned him that the disease could progress in unpredictable ways.

Miles felt a familiar ache catch in his chest. "We never came here, Dad. We only came to this beach once—after ..."

Arthur frowned slightly. "Right. Of course. You were afraid of the water that day."

Miles shook his head gently. Now more than ever, it was the simple places that held the most weight—the ones he never thought would matter, until they did. "We never swam here. You're thinking of Eagle Lake, remember? That's where you taught me to swim."

"Right, right." Arthur paused, running a hand over a piece of driftwood. "Good days and bad days."

Over the years, Miles had learned to wait. His dad's thoughts surfaced on their own time, and rushing them only left them both frustrated.

Arthur straightened, letting the driftwood fall. "It's not your fault, son."

"What do you mean?"

"The fire. Your mom ..." Arthur turned to him. "You were just a kid."

Miles swallowed hard against the tightness in his throat. This wasn't a topic they'd discussed—not even before the Alzheimer's. That night had always been a dividing line in their lives: before and after.

"I know, Dad."

But he didn't know. Not really. Inside him still lived that ten-year-old boy—the one who'd felt his mom pushing him out the bedroom window, her final act before the ceiling collapsed.

Miles shoved his hands into his pockets and felt the familiar spiral shell. He ran his thumb over its ridged surface. Sometimes, he'd hold it up to his ear, swearing he heard something beyond the ambient sounds or the rush of blood in his ears—something calming.

Back at the station, the guys never let him forget his "lucky charm." Once, on the way to a warehouse fire, Bryan had caught Miles rubbing it and asked, "What's the shell saying?"

Tom had chimed in, "I'll bet five bucks that shell's getting more action than we all have this week."

Jeff had simply smiled, lifting his jacket collar to reveal the St. Florian medal tucked beneath. "We all got something."

Miles cleared his throat. "We should go. It's dark."

Arthur nodded, but didn't move. "Five more minutes—to look at the stars."

"Of course, Dad."

It was such a normal request—just like the dad who'd once kept him up past midnight to watch the Braves finish a 12-2 blowout, insisting with that stubborn grin, "You never know what might happen till it's over."

A breeze shifted, carrying a sound—a splash? A muffled voice? Miles glanced down the shoreline, but saw nothing.

Probably just the wind.

As they marveled at the stars, movement down the beach caught Mile's eye—a small, dark shape.

A shorebird?

Then the shadow moved toward them at full tilt—too fast for a bird.

Within seconds, a dog had reached them, circling Arthur's legs before plopping down at his feet.

"Well, hello there, little guy!" Arthur crouched without his usual difficulty, extending his hand. "Where'd you come from?"

The small black dog, with neatly trimmed hair, sniffed cautiously before pressing into Arthur's palm. Then, with a wiggle, the dog flopped onto his back, paws batting at the air, belly on full display.

Arthur chuckled, rubbing the dog's belly. "Aren't you the friendly one?"

Miles smiled, watching his dad interact with the dog as easily as breathing.

It reminded him of the woman from the support group, who'd mentioned bringing her cat to visit her husband in memory care. The facilitator had nodded, explaining how Alzheimer's patients often connected with animals in ways they struggled to with people. "No expectations," she'd said. "Just the present moment."

Miles hadn't gone back after that first meeting. He told himself it was scheduling, but each Wednesday evening when seven o'clock approached, he'd find himself lingering at the kitchen table, car keys in hand, unable to move. Hearing others' stories had left him raw for days. Besides, wasn't he handling things fine? He had systems in place: daily phone calls, charts, medication schedules, and a neighbor who checked on him a few times a week. What good would sitting in a circle of strangers do for either of them?

And yet, watching his dad with Max made something shift inside him. Maybe there were other strategies he could try, like those therapy dog programs the facilitator had recommended.

Kneeling, Miles checked the collar, finding a silver shell-shaped tag with a name and phone number etched on it. "Max," he read aloud, glancing at his dad.

"Max," Arthur repeated, scratching the dog's ears. "Good name for a good boy."

Miles patted his back pocket for his phone, then remembered he'd left it charging on his nightstand. He glanced back at the darkening beach. If they didn't head back soon, the walk home could get twice as difficult. His dad's confusion sometimes worsened after sunset—Dr. Mendez called it "sundowning." But Max clearly belonged to someone who was likely worried sick.

He scanned the area, but no one was in sight. The distant cottages along the shore showed only a handful of scattered lights.

Leave Dad alone while I run for my phone? Not an option.
Bring Max back to the house? Better.

As Miles reached for the dog, the wind carried a faint rustle—then a woman's voice. "Max! Max, where are you?"

5

Wendi

"Max!"

Wendi's pulse roared in her ears as she sprinted down the beach, sand shifting beneath her feet.

In her view, Max twirled in excited circles, his tail a blur. Two men stood beside him—one slightly hunched, the other with his hat pulled low, shadowing his face.

"There you are." She skidded to a breathless stop. Her lungs burned. "Been looking for—almost an hour."

The younger man turned. "He found us," he said. "Just trotted up like he knew where he was going."

She stepped forward, expecting Max to bolt toward her. He didn't move an inch. Instead, he leaned into the older man's leg. He crouched and his fingers found that magic spot behind Max's ears that made his little leg kick like a wind-up toy.

This is the same dog who loses his mind over the UPS guy?

She blinked. Two years, and Max had never taken to anyone like this.

"I'm Wendi." She ran a hand through her wind-tangled hair. "Thanks for keeping an eye on him."

"Miles." His rough hand clasped hers. "And my dad, Arthur."

Arthur pushed himself up with a grunt. "So, you're Max's mom. You've got a good boy here."

"He's usually wary of strangers," she said. "Takes his time with people."

"Guess I passed the test." Arthur chuckled, rubbing Max's head. "Painted a few dogs in my day—one looked a lot like him. Never could quite get fur right. Always ended up looking like a botched haircut. What breed is he, by the way?"

"He's a Yorkipoo. And you paint?"

"Since before Miles was born. Been coming here since—"

Miles stepped in. "We should get going before it gets too dark."

"Yeah, time to get this escape artist home." She clipped the leash onto his collar, bracing for the usual game of keep-away. He stood still, perfectly behaved.

Who are these people, and what have they done to my dog?

Arthur touched Miles's arm. "Your mom always loved the—"

"The beach," Miles finished. "Dad remembers everything about this place."

Wendi nodded. "You from around here?"

"Dad's got a place down the way." Miles pointed vaguely along the shoreline. "I'm from Atlanta. Just here for a bit."

"And you?" Arthur asked.

"Born here. Spent twenty-seven years in Manhattan—big job, big city-life, the whole deal. Then last year ..." She let out a slow breath. "This town called me back."

Arthur's eyes crinkled. "Always does."

"I run an art shop in town—The Painted Shell, off the corner of Main and Maple. Friday's classes are free if you ever feel like dropping in."

"The Painted Shell. Good name." Arthur placed a hand on his chin. "I think my neighbor mentioned that place a time or two. I usually don't go that far—no need."

"I order supplies online for him. It's just easier that way," Miles explained.

Wendi smiled. "First class is on the house," she said, hoping it didn't reek of desperation.

Too late.

Arthur's grin widened. "New brushes wouldn't hurt."

Miles rocked back on his heels. "Maybe we'll swing by sometime. Good meeting you, Wendi."

"Y'all too." The word slipped out before she could stop it. She probably hadn't said "y'all" since the day she'd left Hadley Cove over twenty years before.

As they turned to go, Max strained at the leash, letting out a low, pleading whine.

Arthur kneeled, cupping Max's face. "Kindred souls always recognize each other, don't they, boy?"

6

Miles

Monday

Smoke clogged his lungs. Flames devoured the walls. The hall-way stretched impossibly long.

"Mom!"

A faint cough—somewhere ahead.

He pushed forward, the heat searing his skin.

Then—there. Her silhouette against the inferno, reaching for him—

Above, a loud crack echoed. Embers rained down.

"Miles, now!" Her hands clamped onto his shoulders. "Go!"

"No! Mom, come with me!"

"I'm right behind you! Don't worry!"

A final shove—the heat vanished instantly. Cold air rushed around him as he tumbled through the window. Behind him, a deafening crash.

The house caved in, fire swallowing it whole.

"Mom!"

Miles shot awake, tangled in the sheets, his heart pounding as sweat dripped from his neck.

Is that smoke?

He vaulted upright.

Not smoke ... burned toast.

From the kitchen, the usual morning noises drifted in—cabinets opening, water running, a spoon clinking against ceramic.

"Dad?" He swung his legs over the side of the bed, blinking away the remnants of the dream as the light of the room came into focus.

No answer.

Miles scrubbed a hand over his face, then grabbed a T-shirt from his duffel. He pulled it over his head, still half-asleep as he shuffled down the hall.

Good grief, what happened in here?

The kitchen looked like a war zone—toast crumbs scattered across the counter, coffee forming a small lake on the laminate, chunks of grapefruit pulp floating in puddles of pink juice that had escaped from an overturned pitcher. And in the middle of it all stood his dad, fully dressed in a button-up and pressed khakis, silver hair combed neatly to the side.

"Morning." Arthur grinned. "Made breakfast."

Miles eyed the blackened toast. "Yeah, I can see that."

"We need to get going," Arthur said, sliding a plate of charred toast over.

Miles blinked, feeling like he'd stepped into a sitcom.

"Going where?"

"The Painted Shell." Arthur sipped his coffee like this made perfect sense. "Redhead with the dog?"

Miles stared. His dad remembered Wendi, but he couldn't remember where the bathroom was after asking three times last night.

"I hope they've got good brushes." Arthur drained his mug in one gulp. "And I want to check out that class she mentioned."

Miles had planned to tackle the jungle in the front yard and sort through the stack of mail on the table. But seeing his dad dressed and ready—it was the most present he'd been since Miles had arrived.

"Alright." Miles sighed. "Let me shower first."

By mid-morning, they were meandering down Main Street, the sun warming their faces. For a while, neither of them spoke—just walked side by side, taking in the salty scent of the sea mixed with the smell of freshly baked bread. It was the kind of morning that made the town feel like it belonged on a postcard.

"Morning, Tom," Arthur called to a man sweeping outside the bakery. "Knee any better?"

"Better when I don't think about it!" Tom called back with a hearty laugh, leaning on his broom. "Good to see you, Arthur. Don't be a stranger now."

"You know I can't stay away from your sourdough. Until next time," Arthur said, waving.

They continued along the cobblestone, passing Coastal Creations with its window display of handmade jewelry, then Sarah's Sweets, where saltwater taffy sat alongside sugar cookies shaped like starfish, seashells, and sand dollars.

At a storefront with people on colorful mats visible through the windows, Arthur stopped.

"Hmm. Yoga by the Sea," Miles said, squinting at the sign.

Arthur huffed. "People pay to stretch now?"

Miles bit back a smile, then they strolled down to the corner of Main and Maple where a coral building with a hand painted sign came into view: *The Painted Shell.* Sunlight glinted off the large front windows, where art supplies and coastal-inspired paintings were carefully arranged. Beneath one window, a wooden bench invited passersby to sit, watch the town go by, or maybe linger just a little longer.

Miles hesitated.

What if Wendi was just being nice? What if dad has a meltdown inside? What if—

"Come on." Arthur was already tugging the door open.

A small brass bell chimed as they stepped inside. It smelled like cinnamon and vanilla, with a hint of coffee drifting from behind the counter. Barely audible classical music played from somewhere above. The shop was small but felt unexpectedly airy, thanks to high ceilings and windows flooding the space with sunlight. Every inch of the walls were put to use—paints arranged by color, brushes sorted by type, papers organized by weight and texture. A small gallery space showcased local art, while the back section held tables—likely for the classes.

Arthur made a beeline for the watercolors while Miles hung back. He noticed his dad pause in front of an easel displaying a seascape. After putting on his reading glasses, Arthur moved around it, examining the painting from different angles. When he made a full circle, he let his hand hover inches from the canvas, tracing the brushstrokes in the air. For a moment, Arthur looked like his old self—alive in the way he'd once been when art had been his life.

The sudden scrabble of paws against wood yanked Miles from his thoughts. His eyes darted to a cushioned bed near the window, which Max launched himself off and tore across the shop.

Miles braced himself, but the Yorkipoo blew right past him, circling Arthur's legs with his tail swishing so hard his entire back end shook. The sight reminded him of his fully restored '66 Pontiac GTO fishtailing around corners when he'd been in high school.

Arthur kneeled, scratching behind Max's ears. "Hey there, little fella. Remember me?"

"Oh!" a voice called from behind a curtain. "I thought I heard the bell."

Wendi emerged, arms full of sketchbooks tied with twine. Her red hair was pulled back in a messy ponytail, with strands hanging around her face. A smudge of blue paint marked her forearm. Her cheeks flushed as she spotted them.

"You actually showed up," she said, wearing faded jeans and a green T-shirt that made her eyes—and the freckles across her nose—stand out even more.

"We said we might," Miles said with a wink.

Did I really just wink?

He fought back a face-palm before realizing how different she looked in daylight—softer somehow. Prettier even. Gorgeous actually. It made him wonder what else there was to her he hadn't noticed the first time ...

No, Miles. Stop.

"So the brushes ..." Arthur straightened. "The, uh ... you know, the—" He snapped his fingers. "Kolinsky sables with the red handles. You have those?"

Wendi's eyebrows lifted. "Actually, everything here is vegan—you know, cruelty-free," she said, opening a glass case and sliding out a drawer. "These came in last week. They mimic the same spring and control."

Arthur plucked one of the brushes, bending the bristles. "Huh. Wouldn't have known the difference."

"Exactly. I never felt right about animals being harmed for art supplies—or anything else, really, even if it's been the standard forever."

"Don't like the idea of animals being harmed either." Arthur shook his head. "Never thought about it that way before." He turned the brush over in his hand, seeming to examine it with a new appreciation. "Guess an old dog can still learn new tricks."

Miles smiled and wandered over to the gallery wall. The paintings on it varied—some looked like they belonged in a museum, while others like someone was still figuring things out.

In the center, a beach scene drew his attention: the waves were a little too bright, the sky unnaturally blue, but the piece had a certain joy about it. Next to it, a still life of oranges in a bowl was so realistic, Miles almost thought he could smell the citrus. Another piece was more abstract—bold streaks of red and gold twisting across the canvas like fallen autumn leaves swept up in a breeze. He wasn't sure if that had been the intent, but it worked. A few paintings had tiny yellow price tags on the corners.

Whoa. Do people really pay that much for this stuff?

When he glanced back, he noticed Wendi staring. She quickly tucked a loose strand of hair behind her ear, then shifted her focus to his dad. "These are beautiful," she said, flipping through a small sketchbook Arthur had pulled from his pocket. "You really capture the movement in the water."

"Been painting that cove forever," Arthur said. "Got stacks of paintings back home. Every season, every kind of weather. Even snow on the beach. Now *that'd* be a sight."

"Really?" Wendi's eyes widened. "I'd love to see them."

Miles tensed.

His dad's paintings were strewn about the beach house in various states. Some showed flashes of his old talent. Others were disjointed compositions, strange color choices, and sections left unfinished where it seemed he'd forgotten what he was doing.

"Actually," Wendi said, setting the sketchbook down, "I'm hosting an art auction this Wednesday. Local artists are donating pieces to support our community programs." She gestured toward the class area. "And, honestly, this shop needs—"

"I'll be more than glad to donate some paintings, young

lady," Arthur said.

"That would be incredible." Wendi stepped forward and gave Arthur a quick hug. "Thank you. Thank you so much!"

"It's nothing. Got plenty of them collecting dust." Arthur patted her on the back. "Art's meant to be shared."

Miles opened his mouth to intervene, but stopped himself. A part of him wanted to shield his dad from potential embarrassment. The other part couldn't ignore how *alive* Arthur seemed in that moment. He couldn't bring himself to say anything.

"The auction's Wednesday evening," Wendi said, glancing between them. "But we could look at the paintings before then? I could help select pieces that might work well."

"We'd need to sort through them first," Miles said.

Wendi nodded. "Of course. No pressure."

She rang up Arthur's selections—two brushes, a tube of cobalt blue, a small watercolor pad—while Arthur leaned over, letting Max lick his hand.

"Oh, almost forgot!" Wendi said, giving Arthur his change. "We've got an open class today at three. Super casual, with a few others. You'd be more than welcome." Her eyes flickered to Miles. "Both of you."

Me too?

For a moment, their eyes locked and his pulse quickened.

Miles cleared his throat. "We'll see how the day goes."

Arthur tucked his purchases into the canvas bag Wendi had provided and turned to Miles. "I'd like to come, son," he said quietly, his voice filled with a new sense of purpose. "Been too long since I painted with other people."

As their gazes met, Miles felt his chest tighten. In his

dad's eyes, he glimpsed a spark that had been missing for months. Maybe today wasn't about finding new brushes. Maybe it was about finding the right moment—the one that could help his dad feel like himself again, even if only for a little while.

Miles held the door open, the bell jingling behind them as they left. Through the window, he caught Wendi watching them. He stared—just a beat too long—before turning away.

"Nice lady," Arthur commented, shooting a wayward look at Miles as they walked back up Main Street. "Knows her stuff."

"Yeah, she does."

"Pretty too." Arthur nudged him. "Maybe too pretty for this town."

Miles smirked, keeping his eyes ahead. "So, you think the class is a good idea?"

7

Wendi

WHERE'S EVERYONE AT?

Wendi had lined up the brushes, adjusting each until the bristles pointed in the same direction. Four spots, ready. Water cups filled to the rim. Palettes set with fresh paint. Everything in place ... except the people.

She checked the clock: 2:53 p.m.

Class starts at three.

Max snored softly in his window bed, paws twitching at whatever he was chasing in his dreams. Outside, clouds moved in over the water.

Wendi rolled her shoulders, pressing her fingers into the tight muscle near her neck. Across the room, Wednesday's auction blared from the calendar in thick, red ink. It'd be her last chance to save The Painted Shell. And beneath it, Laurel's offer in blue:

- *Fewer hours*

- *More money*

- *Benefits*

- *Vacation time*

- *Stability*

Less than two weeks to decide between chasing the dream that kept her awake at night or accepting the steady paycheck that might finally let her get some rest.

The bell over the door jangled, startling her. She looked up, pasting on her customer smile. Arthur stepped inside, clutching a canvas bag. Miles followed behind—

No hat this time?

Without it, his brown eyes were darker, more intense, scanning the shop with a quiet focus. His sandy-blond hair curled at the ends. And the way his T-shirt stretched across his chest and arms? Yeah, she was absolutely, definitely not looking.

Heat crept up her neck.

"You made it," she said, then cleared her throat. "Both of you."

"Had to hurry getting groceries." Arthur huffed. "Self-checkout almost made us late. I don't get it—used to be their job to scan everything."

Miles smirked. "Dad, it's not that bad."

"It is when I'm doing the work for free." Arthur shook his head. "This generation will be the end of us, I'm telling you."

Wendi bit her lip. "Well, the good news is you two saved me from talking to myself all afternoon." She gestured at the empty tables. "Looks like it's just us."

From the corner of her eye, she saw Max spring up from his bed. He bounded straight past Wendi and launched himself at Arthur, pawing at his shins.

"Hey, buddy." Arthur chuckled, steadying himself as Max danced on his hind legs. "Ready to paint?"

"I've got a spot for you," Wendi said, leading them to the north-facing windows.

Arthur settled in, unpacking his bag. Miles grabbed a stool and set it against the wall, close enough to observe but still keeping his distance.

"Today's theme is seascapes," Wendi said, laying out some reference photos. "But I'm guessing this isn't new to you."

"Painted more of these than I can count." Arthur tested his brush. "The ocean's never still long enough to get it right."

"That's exactly what makes it challenging." She leaned in, tapping the reference photo. "See how the foam isn't actually white? The sky, the water—it all bleeds into it. That's what makes it look real."

Arthur squinted. "Always struggled with that part."

"Try this." Wendi picked up a fine brush, demonstrating on a scrap of paper. "Instead of painting the foam directly, paint the shadows around it first. Then use your lightest color with the tip of the brush—almost dry—and let the texture of the paper do some of the work."

Arthur raised his eyebrows. "Huh. Never thought of approaching it backward like that."

"It's like negative space. Your brain fills in what the brush hints at. Less is more with white water."

Arthur followed her lead. A few strokes, a smudged shadow—suddenly, the foam lifted from the page. He sat back with a satisfied smile. "Well, I'll be. That does look better." His hands continued moving, and within minutes, he'd blocked in a horizon and waves that seemed to move on the paper.

She let out a low whistle. "You just did that. Like it was nothing."

"I suppose I did," Arthur said, adding a streak of yellow where the sun hit the water. "Looks more alive now."

She nodded, then glanced up to find Miles watching them. Their eyes met across the room, and he leaned forward and rested his forearms on his knees. Her stomach dipped.

Of course. Just my luck.

She resisted the urge to check if her bun had fallen apart like it always did by mid-afternoon. The thrifted T-shirt she'd thrown on this morning now felt too casual—especially with the coffee stain she really hoped he hadn't noticed.

I should've put on mascara.

Wendi turned back to Arthur. "You really have been doing this for a long time. This looks amazing."

"Still got it in me. At least most of it."

As Arthur painted, Max settled beside his chair, resting on his shoe.

"Your water's looking murky," she said, reaching for his cup. "Let me refresh that for you."

"Yeah, that'd be great," he said without looking up.

With Arthur settled with clean water, she made her way to the kitchenette, keeping an eye on him from across the room. "Coffee?" she asked Miles.

He glanced up from his phone. "Yeah, thanks."

She poured two mugs, adding a splash of cream to hers. When she passed him his, their fingers brushed—for a second.

Did he notice that? Or was it just me?

"He's incredible," she said. "Most people overthink it."

"Funny thing is, he never had any formal training. He worked at a plant—random shifts, long hours." He took a sip. "But any free time he had, he was painting. Studying. Figuring it out on his own."

"That's even more impressive," she said, leaning against the counter. "You can't teach that kind of instinct. Some people take classes for years and never get where he is."

Miles stood as he looked toward his dad, then back at her. "Yeah, he's gifted for sure."

"What about you? Do you paint?"

He huffed a laugh. "Now that's funny."

"No creative side at all?"

"Nah, sports were more my thing—football, baseball, wrestling, track. Tried a little of everything."

"Ah, so you were a jock," she said, giving his arm a light slap. The moment her hand met solid muscle, something electric and entirely inconvenient ricocheted up her arm. "I mean, obviously, right? You've got the build for it."

Miles chuckled. "Not like I use to. But years of sports, and then firefighting helped. Keeps you in decent shape."

Decent?

"Firefighter?" She straightened. "Really?"

Something crossed his face—something she couldn't quite name. But somehow, all at once, it said everything and nothing. "Used to be."

The conversation stalled.

"Had a panic attack. Froze up. My partner had to pull me out."

"I'm so sorry."

He shrugged. "It's okay. Resigned after and been doing odd jobs since—construction, dog walking, and yard work. Whatever I can find."

"That why you're back here?"

"Part of it." His eyes went to Arthur then back to her. "He got diagnosed with Alzheimer's a couple years back. Yesterday, his neighbor called me at two in the morning. Found him wandering the beach in his pajamas." He tapped his thumb against his mug, once, twice, before exhaling. "Has his good days, good moments. And bad ones."

She hesitated before resting a hand on his forearm. "That must be hard."

His gaze flicked to where she touched him and he gave her a small, lopsided smile. "Yeah. But he still paints. Seems to help."

She returned the smile, pulling her hand back. "He's lucky to have you."

"Just doing what I have to."

The simplicity of his words sent a warmth through her bones.

For a beat, they just stood there. Wendi found herself studying the curve of Miles' jaw. When she realized she was staring, she set her mug down. "So ... dog walking, huh?"

"What? That surprises you?"

"Just trying to picture you wrangling a pack of poodles."

"Word on the street is that I'm the best dog walker east of the Mississippi," he said, grinning now.

"Oh, is that so?"

"Definitely. Though, between us, I think they walked me more than I walked them."

"Somehow I doubt that." Wendi chuckled, shaking her head. "We should probably check on your dad."

When they returned, Arthur was putting the final touches on a scene so striking that Wendi froze mid-step.

He'd captured the light filtering around storm clouds, with one patch of ocean lit up while everything else remained in shadow. A small boat sat on the bright water, its sails standing out against the darker waves around it. It seemed to move, as if the light was pulling it forward through the storm.

"Arthur ... Wow, this is gorgeous," she said.

He looked up. "Not my best work. Nothing like my special project."

"Special project?"

"Been working on it for months," he said. "Most important painting I've ever done. Needs to be perfect."

Wendi caught Miles' raised brow.

News to him too.

"I plan to finish it tomorrow. I've got a nice frame for it too. It'll be ready for the auction."

Wendi smiled. "I can't wait to see it."

Arthur began cleaning his brush. "It's been a lot of fun

here today."

"Yeah, today's flown by," Miles said, examining the painting.

"It really has." Wendi's smile faltered, slightly. "I was thinking about grabbing dinner—feel like joining?"

Arthur shooed them off. "Go on, you kids have fun. I've got a TV dinner and a painting to finish."

"Dad, are you sure?"

"Go, enjoy yourselves," Arthur said as he collected his supplies.

Miles turned to Wendi. "I need to get my dad set up at home. I could meet you there in probably half an hour?"

Just me and Miles?

A date?

No—well, maybe?

Just two ... friends? Acquaintances with ... potential?

Breathe, girl. It's only dinner.

"Yeah, let's do that," she said, impressed by how casual her voice sounded despite her quickening pulse.

She watched as Miles helped gather his dad's things, offering a few parting words and a brief smile to Arthur. As they headed for the door, Wendi released a sigh. There was something about watching Miles walk away that made her realize how much she wanted him to stay.

Max trotted alongside the guys, tail wagging with such hope that Wendi almost felt guilty keeping him from an adventure he clearly thought he deserved. "Max, I'm sorry, boy," she said, scooping him up.

Miles grinned, reaching over to give Max a pat. "We'll see you again soon."

Arthur nodded at the dog. "You keep an eye on things here, okay?"

Once they'd left, she set Max down and blew out a breath. One thought hit: *What the heck am I wearing?*

Red top? Too formal.

Teal V-neck? Still too much.

Hmm. What if I wear it with jeans?

When was the last time she'd worried this much about what to wear? High school? College? That blind date a year ago that had ended with her eating dessert alone?

Ugh, why is this so hard?

Wait. Would changing be weird? Or would not changing be worse?

They'd already seen her in this outfit. Changing now would make it look like she was trying too hard—like it was a date. Was it? No, she was probably overthinking it. Again.

But she could at least freshen up her makeup. Or would that be too obvious? It was just a normal dinner. With a sweet man who'd left Atlanta to take care of his dad. With a man whose arms had no right being that distracting.

The door swung open.

Miles reappeared, one hand braced on the frame. "Sorry, where'd you say we're meeting?"

8

Miles

MILES PROPPED HIMSELF UP against a streetlamp outside Phil's Diner. A neon sign hummed above, throwing a red glow onto the sidewalk as the breeze carried salt and the smoky scent of grilled onions and fries.

His fingers brushed over the spiral shell in his pocket, tracing its familiar ridges. He'd been standing here for fifteen minutes already, still not entirely sure what to call this evening with Wendi. Not a date, exactly—they hadn't used that word. Just dinner. Simple enough. But that didn't explain the nervous energy coursing through him or why he'd changed shirts twice before leaving.

Whatever this was, dating hadn't exactly been a highlight reel lately. There was the Atlanta fitness influencer who'd mistaken their date for a podcast monologue. And the woman from the bar who'd lost interest the second she'd realized he wasn't fighting fires anymore. And he couldn't forget the lady from the app who'd turned from charming to concerning—showing up at his apartment unannounced after he'd bailed twice, then flooding his phone with messages for weeks after.

He checked his phone again—7:15.

Maybe she changed her mind?

Just as he turned to leave, Wendi hurried up the sidewalk, cheeks flushed and slightly breathless.

"Sorry I'm late," she said, sweeping stray strands of hair behind her ear. "Max wasn't having it when he saw me getting ready. Hid under the bed until I bribed him with treats—then made a break for it the second I opened the door."

She'd changed into a green dress, fitted just enough to make him aware of her figure, while her hair tumbled in loose red waves around her shoulders. Wendi wasn't just beautiful. She was the kind of beautiful that made a man forget whatever he'd been thinking a second ago.

And here I am, looking like I just came off a three-day camping trip. Great.

Miles opened his mouth, then stopped.

Cute? Too casual.

Pretty? Maybe.

Gorgeous? Definitely too much.

He cleared his throat. "You clean up good."

"Thanks." She looked downward. "I don't usually dress up much these days."

Miles glanced at his flannel and jeans, then shrugged. "It's the fanciest outfit I packed."

"Flannel works." Her smile did something weird to his collar—tightened it, somehow.

They stood there for a moment—that split second of not being sure whether to hug, shake hands, or go inside. Miles chose to open the door.

Inside, Phil's Diner delivered what the name promised—checkered floors, red vinyl booths, and a vintage jukebox spinning the latest Taylor Swift hit. The walls were lined with photos showing Hadley Cove throughout the decades.

Miles's attention drifted to a picture from the early 2000s—an old storefront, now a hardware store, draped with banners for a town fair. Another captured a community fundraiser, a row of wagging tails barely peeking into the frame. A third showed a school field day: kids in oversized T-shirts, mid-laugh as they dodged water balloons, while parents stood nearby with plates of food. Off to the side, a burly man worked the grill, dishing out burgers from a steaming tray.

"Red!" A mountain of a man in a white apron approached, arms outstretched and a wide smile on his face. "Well, look at you—mighty fancy tonight."

"Something like that," Wendi said with a grin. "Phil, this is Miles."

Phil shook Miles's hand with a firm grip. "Any friend of Wendi's is welcome here." He led them to a corner booth, wiping the table, before his eyes landed on Wendi. "The usual?"

"Actually, let's do the Beyond Burger instead of the Impossible one. And I'll swap the Dr. Pepper for a vanilla oat milkshake."

"Switching it up on me, I see." Phil turned to Miles. "And

for you, son?"

Miles scanned the menu, his eyes darting from one item to the next.

"Ah, you're looking at the breakfast-for-dinner specials?" Phil asked. "Well, if you're gonna do it, you might as well go all in. Try the pumpkin spice pancakes. They come with a seasonal syrup and a coffee to match. It's the Fall favorite."

Miles nodded, smiling. "That sounds great."

"Good to see Wendi Parker finally letting a man take her out," Phil called over his shoulder as he walked away.

Wendi rolled her eyes. "He's been on a mission to find me a man ever since I moved back."

"Any luck?"

"Not yet," she said with a smirk, leaning back in the booth.

Miles smiled and tilted his head. "So, 'Red?'"

"Had the hair since birth, so people got lazy with nicknames around here."

Phil returned with their drinks. "How's the little trouble-maker doing? When do we get to see him again?"

Wendi shot him a pointed look. "You remember what happened last time ..."

Phil waved her off. "Max is always welcome here."

Miles raised an eyebrow. "What happened?"

"Max swiped Mrs. Peterson's biscuit straight off her plate. Then ran laps like he'd won the Super Bowl while half the diner chased him."

"A little chaos never hurt anyone." Phil chuckled. "Besides, business was slow that day—gave us something to talk about for weeks. Anyway, I'll be back with your orders in a jiff!"

As Phil walked away, Miles sipped his coffee. "How long have you been back?"

"A little over a year." She stirred her shake with the straw. "Made one call to the bank, got approved, and the shop was opened a few weeks later."

"Bold move. One phone call and you got a store? Last time I tried that, I only got a pizza."

The corner of Wendi's mouth quirked upward. "So tell me something random about you. Can be anything."

Miles leaned back, pretending to consider. "Easy one—I hate beer. Can't do it. I always end up ordering fruity drinks instead."

"No way! Same. People swear it's an acquired taste, but I'm pretty sure that's a lie."

"Right? I can handle shots, no problem. But beer? Yeah, that's a no-go for me."

"Me too. Hate it … Okay, I have an idea. On three, say your favorite drink. Ready?"

"Alright."

Wendi counted down. "Three … two … one …"

"Tequila Sunrise," they both blurted at the exact same time. Then blinked.

"I knew there was a reason I liked you," she said.

"Same. We're getting them sometime soon."

"Deal," she said, as her gaze locked onto his.

Phil reappeared, setting down a towering stack of pancakes for Miles and a burger with golden fries for Wendi. "Enjoy, y'all."

Miles cut into his pancakes, took a bite, and closed his

eyes. "Okay, these pancakes might be life-changing."

"Of course." Wendi groaned as a drop of milkshake hit her dress. "Can't take me anywhere."

Without thinking, he slid his napkin across the table toward her. Their fingers brushed, and he caught himself studying the curve of her neck where it met her shoulder.

At that moment, Taylor Swift's "This is Why We Can't Have Nice Things" started playing on the jukebox. Wendi pointed at the speaker, and they both burst out laughing.

"Can't make this up," Miles said.

Wendi dramatically mouthed along with the chorus, and Miles joined in, using his spoon as an impromptu microphone. A few other diners glanced their way, but they were too busy to care, trying to outdo each other with increasingly ridiculous facial expressions as they silently performed the song.

After the bridge, Miles set the spoon down. "If it's any consolation, you still look great, milkshake and all."

"Thanks. I guess it's not too obvious." Wendi set the napkin down. "You know, I used to stress about stuff like this all the time. My ex always wanted me dressed up for something. Corporate dinners, networking events, designer everything. But mainly for him. Heaven forbid I decided not to wear makeup."

"Sounds exhausting."

"It was. And juggling that with my PR job at Pinnacle Hotels? Pure misery."

Miles leaned in. "What made you finally leave the job?"

She ran a fingertip along the rim of her glass. "Well ... I was in the middle of a presentation to forty executives, explaining our rebrand strategy, and out of nowhere, my hands started shaking. I couldn't get the words out. I tried to push through, but it kept getting worse. Before I knew it, I was hyperventilating in the bathroom while my assistant called 911." She paused, releasing a deep breath. "It was like everything hit me all at once. I realized I couldn't keep living like that." She looked up. "Sorry for the trauma dump."

"No, don't be sorry. I asked because I wanted to know. You've been through a lot, Wendi."

"Oh, the saga continues. James filed for divorce two months later. Said he 'hadn't signed up for this.' After that, I returned to Hadley Cove with nothing but Max and the dream of being an art store owner."

"How long have you had Max?"

"About two years now. Got him during the divorce. He was at the city shelter. They found him after some kids had been throwing rocks at him. He was there for months and was scheduled to be euthanized. I happened to see him online and went in just in time ..." She shook her head. "Those eyes. It was like we recognized each other. Like we were meant to be together, you know?"

Miles nodded. "You both needed each other."

"Exactly. He stayed by my side through everything." A flicker of a smile passed across Wendi's lips. "And now he apparently loves your dad more than me. Ungrateful."

"Nah, but it kind of does look that way." His tone shifted. "Thanks for sharing all that. I know it doesn't always feel like it, but your best days haven't even happened yet. At least, that's what I keep telling myself."

Her eyes twinkled as they met his with a quiet intensity.

The moment broke when an elderly woman appeared beside their table. "Wendi Parker! Why haven't you introduced me to your handsome friend here?"

Wendi grinned. "How rude of me. Ada, this is Miles. Miles, Ada Harrison."

Ada sported an orange velvet blazer over an ivory silk blouse. Wide-legged pants, sleek black heels, a strand of pearls, and diamond studs. A vintage flower brooch perched on her lapel, while oversized sunglasses sat atop her wild, snowy-white hair.

"Mind if I join y'all?" She didn't wait for an answer before sliding in beside Wendi.

"So, Miles"—Ada leaned forward—"where's home? And what brings you to our town?

"Atlanta. Here to help my dad out for a while."

"And who might your father be?"

"Arthur Dalton."

"Oh, Arthur, the painter!" Ada clasped her hands together. "I see him nearly every morning during my beach walks. Always so focused, he barely notices me waving."

"That's him. I'm sure he doesn't mean to—"

"Though I must say,"—she eyed Miles's arms—"Arthur's talented, but he doesn't have those."

Miles chuckled. "Thanks."

She patted Wendi's hand. "Good choice, dear. Good choice, indeed."

Wendi blushed. "We're just friends."

"Oh, they always start as 'just friends.' And I might just make an appearance at your 'Save the Shell' auction Wednesday. Had no clue how much trouble your shop was in. If you'd mentioned it sooner, I could've made a call—gotten that rent lowered in no time. Or at least, rounded up more of the ladies from the club to visit your little art store."

Wendi pressed her lips together.

As Ada rose, she circled the table and pulled Miles into a hug that smelled strongly of gardenias and potpourri. The embrace lingered well past the point of comfort and she gave his bicep a quick squeeze before finally releasing him. "Have any of the men in Hadley Cove even heard of a pushup? Apparently, Miles has."

She turned to Wendi, wrapping her into an equally suffocating hug. "Don't let this one get away, dear."

As soon as Ada was out of earshot, they both exhaled a small laugh.

"What was that?" Miles asked.

"That's Ada for you. You're officially a local now."

"She's something, that's for sure." He paused as his pulse ticked up—nothing dramatic, but enough that he felt it.

Just ask.

Miles let out a steady breath, hoping to keep his voice even. "Want to come by tonight? Help pick out some paintings for the auction?"

9

Wendi

Wendi eased her car behind Miles's truck and cut the engine. A cottage stood outlined against the darkening sky. She slung her purse over her shoulder and stepped out. Shell wind chimes clinked on a porch where a rocking chair sat beside an old cooler. Waves crashed steadily beyond the house.

She followed the sandy path to the porch, barely reaching the welcome mat before Miles pulled open the door.

"Fair warning—this place isn't exactly HGTV material."

"Join the club. My place looks like a tornado went through it."

She walked inside—and froze. Paintings crowded the space, leaning against walls, stacked on tables, propped on chairs. Landscapes, seascapes, and still lifes in watercolor, acrylic, and oil. Between them—pill organizers, sticky-note reminders, and a whiteboard calendar with appointments color-coded.

Arthur stood at an easel by the window. When he saw them, he beamed. "There she is!"

"Hey, Arthur." Wendi stepped closer.

"Ah, ah—no peeking." He shot her a wink. "Big reveal on Wednesday."

"The one you mentioned earlier?"

He dipped his brush in water. "That's the one."

"We should start sorting these if we want to finish tonight," Miles said, motioning toward the stacks.

"Take whatever speaks to you," Arthur said. "Miles knows my best work."

They settled on the floor beside the first stack. Wendi lifted each canvas with care, taking in Arthur's brushwork. Again and again, the cove appeared—dawn, dusk, summer, winter—the same shore, yet captured differently each time.

Their fingers grazed as they reached for the same one. A small spark zipped through her. Wendi glanced up quickly, surprised by how close they were sitting now, knees almost touching.

She cleared her throat. "This one belongs in the auction."

They continued in silence, separating the pieces into piles. Sifting through them, Wendi noticed Miles setting aside certain ones with strange color choices. No comment. No explanation. Just a quiet decision. She told herself it wasn't her business to ask.

Finally, they moved to a collection of still lifes.

Then she saw *it*.

Her breath caught. A small painting of a metal tin with its lid open. Inside, lay a piece of sea glass, a sand dollar, and a shark tooth.

No way.

Her hand hovered over the canvas. "Arthur, what's the story with this one?"

Arthur looked up. "Found it a couple years back, near the cove. Neat tin. Decided to paint it." He stood, moving to a nearby shelf. "Still have it somewhere ..."

He rummaged around briefly before producing it, dented but unmistakable. He cradled it for a moment, almost like a treasure, before opening it. Inside, the contents were exactly as she remembered.

But no spiral shell.

The memory struck with unexpected force. For a moment, she was back there—the boy, the beach, his tear-streaked face, the way he held the shell to his ear.

A voice yanked her back.

"You okay?" Miles asked.

"Just admiring the detail." She managed a smile, though it felt brittle.

She couldn't bring herself to explain—to tell them what the tin had meant, what it had once held, and how it had made her feel. Instead, she watched as Arthur handled it with a tenderness that made her heart ache. It belonged to him now, and she was okay with that.

"Going to read a few chapters of that mystery novel before I turn in," Arthur said, setting the tin back on the shelf.

"Need anything?" Miles asked.

Arthur clasped his son's shoulder as he passed. "I've still got a few good years in me, you know. But don't keep her up too late—you both look like you need some sleep."

After Arthur disappeared down the hallway, they continued sorting through paintings. Wendi caught herself watching Miles—how his lips pressed together when he focused, the faint crease between his brows and the careful, almost reverent way he held each canvas. Her eyes wandered to the scar on his forearm that ran from the crook of his elbow to his wrist.

Without thinking, her fingers moved, reaching out and tracing the scar.

Miles went still. "House fire. I was ten."

She quickly withdrew her hand. "That must've been awful. I'm sorry."

"It's alright. Just one of those things." He reached for another canvas, the topic clearly closed.

She took the hint. "So how'd you end up in Atlanta?"

"Born and raised. Never left." Miles paused, glancing at her, then back to the canvas in his hands. "And you? How'd a small-town girl end up running PR in Manhattan?"

Wendi smiled. The answer felt simple and complicated. "Pure stubbornness. Growing up, all I wanted was out of this town. Funny how life turns out."

"Sounds like the shop brought you back to what you love."

"That was the plan." She leaned back against the couch. "Here's my Hallmark movie pitch: Small-town girl comes home, opens dream business, finds herself again."

"How's that working out for you?"

"Finding myself? Some days, yeah. The business? Not so much. If the auction flops, that's it. I'm done for."

"Then what?"

"My old boss called on Sunday with a job offer. Better hours, more money. Everything I should want ..." Her shoulders slumped.

"But?"

"Leaving feels like giving up." The honesty surprised her. "But staying might be worse. At least financially."

Miles seemed to study her. "Starting over takes guts. Seem's like you've already done the hard part. That's got to count for something."

She tilted her head at his observation, free of judgment or advice. He made it sound so simple.

And just like that, James was in her head. She could almost hear him now, the way he'd leaned across their kitchen island years back when she'd mentioned wanting to leave her job at Pinnacle and open an art store in New York: *"Wendi, you're not thinking this through logically. You need more strategy. There are risks, and I'm not sure you're accounting for them all. Let me explain how a business plan works ..."*

The lectures always came sugarcoated in concern, but beneath that was something condescending, as if he were the only one capable of truly seeing the "right" way to handle things.

"Anything I can do?" Miles asked. "Want help setting up for auction?"

"You don't have to do that."

Miles placed a hand on hers. "I want to."

For a beat, she could only stare at his calloused fingers resting on hers. A slow flutter unfurled in her stomach. He squeezed her hand lightly and the pressure of his fingers seemed to pull her closer, and for a second, she imagined leaning into him, letting the distance between them disappear completely. But then—he let go.

They pressed on, selecting eight paintings for the auction. The process felt almost ritualistic—choosing what would be seen and what would be remembered. Wendi's mind worked methodically as she glanced over each piece.

She picked four of the cove during the day: early morning, midday brightness, late afternoon, and one with a soft storm rolling in. Those would offer a range of moods, she thought—serenity balanced by a bit of drama. Then, another two of the cove, this time at twilight in deep purples and blues—a more romantic feel.

Next, she chose a still life—wildflowers in mason jars, both inviting and personal. To round it out, she picked one of a small boat anchored just off the coast. Its soft pastel colors gave it a dreamlike quality.

Once they were done, Miles gathered the paintings, and they walked out the door toward her car. A canopy of stars shimmered overhead, glinting on the water. With each step, Wendi grew more aware of Miles—his height, the scent of bay rum and cedar, and the way his shoulder brushed hers. She tried to ignore it, but it was *impossible*.

A canvas slipped, and Miles caught it just before it hit the ground. The sudden motion brought them even closer.

Inches.

In the moonlight, his brown eyes gleamed, almost golden.

She couldn't look away. Didn't want to.

His gaze held hers—deep, steady, pulling her in.

Her pulse quickened.

But what? Was he waiting for her?

Her heart raced. Faster. Faster.

Her lips parted—just barely, just enough.

Closer. She could feel the heat of his breath.

And then—

"Miles?" Arthur's voice called from the porch.

They sprang apart.

Wendi nearly tripped over her own feet as she jumped back. She let out a startled laugh that came out higher than intended.

"Did we check the mail today? My magazine should've come by now."

"Yes, Dad, we did. It won't get here until next Monday."

"I do remember you saying that. Well, didn't mean to interrupt. Oh yeah, one more thing. Tomorrow I'm going to show you both where I do my best work. How's three sound, young lady?"

"That sounds perfect," she called back.

Miles sighed, running a hand through his hair. "I should probably—"

"Of course." She busied herself with opening the trunk.

When they finished loading the paintings, Miles shut it. "Glad you came over. Dad seems better when you're around."

"I mean, I am kind of wonderful."

"More than kind of."

She and Miles stood facing each other. What was the protocol here? They weren't colleagues or just friends, but they weren't ... whatever that almost-moment had been.

A hug? Full on or side hug?

A handshake? Please not a handshake.

The air between them felt charged—uncertain, waiting, stretching too long and too short.

Finally, he moved forward and wrapped his arms around her in a brief hug.

"See you tomorrow?" she asked, reluctantly pulling away.

"Yeah. Tomorrow."

She nodded, but didn't step away. Neither did he.

"Well," she said, jingling her keys. "Goodnight, then."

"Goodnight, Wendi."

Another moment passed before he took a backward step toward the house. "Drive safe."

Inside her car, she closed her eyes, tipping her head back against the seat.

Miles.

If Arthur hadn't called his name ...

Her phone chimed, snapping her out of it. The screen glowed in the dark interior.

Laurel: *Need your decision by Friday. The board wants someone this weekend, not the next, like I had said. They have a candidate they want to hire. I told them to wait until I heard back from you. Let me know either way.*

10

Miles

Tuesday

MILES PLACED THE LAST of Arthur's painting supplies into the truck, everything packed with care: brushes sorted by size, paints arranged by color, and canvases tucked into the sleeve he'd found buried in the hall closet.

"We're going to be late," Arthur muttered, pacing beside the truck, eyeing the sky. "Can't miss the light. It's perfect this time of day."

"Almost done." Miles tucked the sunscreen into the side pocket of the supply bag, remembering the time he'd forgotten it on a day cruise in Savannah. His dad's nose had turned lobster-red, and he'd never heard the end of it.

Not going through that again.

He patted his pocket and pulled out the pill organizer, quickly running through it.

Morning pills—taken.
Afternoon pills—done.
Evening pills—here.

Miles snapped the tailgate shut after one last check. He moved to help Arthur into the passenger seat, but his dad waved him off. "I'm not completely useless, you know."

As they drove through town, Miles's mind replayed last night on repeat—the weight of the paintings in his arms, the silver-blue moonlight catching in Wendi's hair, that electric moment when they'd almost …

What was he doing? He didn't want to lead her on—she'd been through enough. Too much. The last thing she needed was him complicating things even more.

He wasn't staying in Hadley Cove long-term—or was he? If he did, he'd still have to hire a full-time caretaker for his dad, eventually, or find a memory care facility.

Dad would never go for that.

Miles's apartment in Atlanta still had his name on the lease. His life was there—or what remained of it, anyway. But last night, the way Wendi had looked at him, so close, so real—it made him question everything.

Could he even give her what she needed?

The station house he'd called home for twenty years, where the rush of adrenaline and the sense of purpose had once been enough to keep him going. Now? He was just a guy with no real direction, doing odd jobs around town and trying to keep his dad's days in order.

Could a man who had lost himself be the person she deserved?

Maybe?

He wasn't sure of anything anymore. But something about Wendi felt … right. He couldn't explain it. It just did, and maybe that was the only answer that mattered.

"You got that look again." Arthur's voice cut through his thoughts.

"What look?"

"Same look your mom used to get when she was over-thinking something." Arthur turned to watch the store-fronts blur past. "Some things don't need all that analysis, son."

Mom.

Even the mention of her, almost four decades later, stirred something inside him he'd rather not revisit. But the salt air seeping through the truck window brought with it the memory of her perfume—something light, oceanic, that she'd always worn. She would've loved this drive. Over the years, he'd learned that the hardest part of holding on was knowing when to let go. And the hardest part of letting go was wondering if he ever really could.

Miles kept his eyes on the road. Some things were better left unsaid.

When The Painted Shell came into view, Miles spotted Wendi on the phone. As they opened the door, Max shot out from behind the counter, weaving between displays before charging straight for Arthur.

"Hey, little fella." Arthur crouched, and Max jumped up, pawing at his chest, his tongue darting to lick his chin.

Wendi ended the call with a swift goodbye, slipping the phone into her pocket as she did. "Hey, you two. I just need to grab my stuff."

Miles leaned against the counter. "Everything okay?"

"Yeah, I'm fine." She kneeled, clipping Max's leash to his vest.

Definitely not fine.

He kept the thought to himself, hesitating before he decided against grabbing her tote. He wasn't sure if she wanted help or space.

Arthur straightened up. "Time to go, kids."

"We know, Dad."

The coastal road narrowed, the pavement giving way to gravel and sand. Miles pulled into a small clearing where the road dead-ended at the dunes.

Wendi climbed out with Max, taking in the surroundings. "Wait, I came here as a kid. We basically drove in a circle." She chuckled and pointed. "Look, my store's right there."

Arthur followed her hand, then shrugged. "Miles knows I'm bad with directions."

Miles grabbed the supplies from the truck bed, biting back a laugh.

The cove unfolded before them—a perfect crescent of sand nestled between rocky outcroppings. Waves rolled in, leaving delicate traces of foam that vanished before they reached the shore. Seagulls cawed overhead, wings cutting graceful arcs through the sky. The air carried the salty scent of the sea, mingling with the faint, earthy aroma of beach grass growing in tufts along the sand. It was quiet—peaceful, as if the world had forgotten this corner of it existed.

Arthur pointed toward a flat stretch where the dunes met the beach. "Right there. That's the spot."

Miles set up the easel, peering over at Wendi. She spread a blanket on the sand, Max trotting over to claim a corner. Pulling out her sketchbook, she began drawing, glancing occasionally at Arthur with something like admiration shining in her eyes.

For a while, Miles just watched them. Wendi's gaze had drifted from the paper back to the water, then back again, while Arthur painted with complete absorption. Life rarely gave Miles the answers he sought, but sometimes it offered perfect moments like this instead—ones that reminded him of who his dad had been and maybe who he still could be.

A light breeze kicked up, ruffling the edge of Wendi's sketchbook. She ran a hand over the page to smooth it, then glimpsed Miles, as if considering something. She sighed, stretching her legs out in front of her and setting her pencil aside.

"Want to take a walk?" Wendi asked, closing her sketchbook.

Miles looked at her, then at his dad. "Yeah. We'll stay close."

Wendi

As Wendi and Miles strolled along the shoreline, Max sprinted ahead, nose to the ground, investigating shells and chasing waves. Then he froze, ears perked, before he started digging away with his paws, sand flying in all directions. With one final scoop, Max pulled something from the hole—a soggy, sand-crusted sock.

"Maximus Parker," Wendi huffed, giving her best *mom* tone. "Drop it."

Max stiffened and dropped the sock at her feet. His eyes darted between the sock and Wendi, wearing a look that was equal parts guilt and triumph.

Miles grinned. "Full government name, huh?"

"Only for the serious infractions," she said, tossing one of Max's toys, watching as he bounded after it. She drew in a deep breath, pulling the crisp salt air into her lungs. "I love November beach days here. Sometimes it's seventy, some days it's forty. We got lucky."

"Yeah, we did." Miles's gaze went to Arthur. "This place meant a lot to my parents. They honeymooned here."

"Great place for one. Not that I'd know—I never got a real honeymoon. There was always some excuse. After a while, I just stopped asking."

"You're in good company. Never made it to a honeymoon," Miles said with a half-smile. "Closest I got was a weekend in Charleston—didn't even make it to check-in."

Wendi chuckled and nudged his arm. "What was growing up in Atlanta like?"

He shrugged. "Pretty normal, I guess. A's and B's in school and tried every sport I could. Mom kept us both in line." He paused, surprised by how easily the forgotten details returned. "After she passed, Dad did his best. Worked crazy hours, but never missed a game or a school thing."

"He really showed up for you."

"Yeah," Miles said, glancing toward Arthur. "He did." After a beat, he turned to her. "What about you? Growing up here—was it always beaches and small-town charm?"

"Not exactly." She traced a slow line in the sand with her toe, watching as the breeze erased it. "I loved it here, but I used to run up to this spot when my parents argued. Which was a lot." She gestured toward the dunes. "I'd bring a sketchbook, sit on the rocks, and draw. The ocean never made me pick a side."

Miles looked out at the water. "Good way to deal with things. Better than how most kids would've handled it."

She shrugged. "It didn't feel like much of a choice. Just the only place that felt right."

Max barked—sharp, sudden. They turned to see him

standing over a tide pool, ears flattened, barking at his own reflection.

"First time seeing himself from there?" Miles grinned.

Wendi sighed as Max swiped a paw at the water, splashing his face. "He's his own worst enemy."

With one last snort, Max bolted from the tide pool—charging straight at them. A split second later, he shook himself dry, sending a spray of water over them both.

"Max!" Wendi sputtered, swiping at the cold droplets on her face.

"No government name?"

"Ah, not this time."

Max flopped onto the sand as Wendi and Miles shared an amused glance. As they continued walking, Wendi stopped abruptly, the wind lifting her hair.

"Everything okay?" he asked.

Most people wouldn't have noticed. Not enough to ask, anyway. Plenty of people had known her for years, but few ever looked closely enough to see when something shifted. She was good at brushing things off, at deflecting with a joke or an easy smile. But Miles? He saw her.

She shook her head. "Nothing really. Just ... Laurel texted again. I have to decide by Friday."

"About the New York job?"

She nodded, digging her toes into the sand. "Yeah. I went over everything with her before you picked me up. Financially, it's the smart choice. The right answer."

"And if you turn it down?"

"More than likely, I'll be watching my dream die in slow motion." She gave a small, sad laugh. "Some choice, huh?"

She braced for a well-meaning platitude, the kind she could nod along to and forget. Instead, Miles reached for her hand and her breath hitched as a certain lightness rolled through her, unexpected but not unwelcome. Her heartbeat stuttered, then accelerated as his fingers threaded through hers like they belonged there. She hadn't realized how much she needed this—a simple touch, a quiet reassurance that someone saw her, that someone understood.

"Whatever happens with the shop, you'll figure it out." He squeezed her hand. "We'll figure it out."

Did he just say ...

"*We'll* ... as in us?" The words slipped out. Her pulse jumped.

No taking it back now.

What if she'd read this all wrong?

His thumb traced slow circles over her knuckles. "Yeah. Us."

She let out a slow breath, trying to ground herself in the moment. "I like the sound of 'us.'"

"Me too."

"Total vibe killer," she said with a sheepish smile. "But before I forget—can you make it to the shop around four tomorrow to help set up?"

"Wouldn't miss it." His tone made the practical request feel like anything but a vibe killer.

Hand in hand, they turned back toward Arthur. Max trotted between them, occasionally bumping their legs as he pranced along. But as they drew closer, Wendi noticed a change in Arthur's posture. What had started as a peaceful scene—a man absorbed in his painting, relaxed in the sun—was now something else entirely.

Arthur went rigid, his brushstrokes turning erratic, jerky. The tranquil blues of sky and sea had vanished beneath frenzied streaks of orange-red, clawing across the canvas.

"Dad?" Miles stepped closer. "How's the painting coming along?"

Arthur didn't look up, just kept adding more red-orange, his breathing quick and shallow.

Wendi moved beside Miles, eyes shifting between the painting and Arthur.

Flames?

Arthur muttered something. His brush jabbed at the canvas with frantic urgency. Wendi barely caught the words. Fragments surfaced: "Smoke everywhere. Too late."

A tightness coiled in Wendi's chest.

Poor Arthur.

Miles kneeled beside him. "Dad, we're at the beach. You're painting the cove, remember?"

Arthur's hand trembled, the brush shaking in his grip as his eyes flicked to Wendi. "Elaine? When'd you get here?"

12
Miles

"Dad, that's not Mom. That's Wendi, remember? From the painting class?"

Arthur blinked rapidly, eyes darting from the canvas to Miles, then back again. He shook his head. "I was painting water ... When'd the fire start?"

"It's okay." Miles carefully pried the brush from his dad's trembling hand. "Just got mixed up for a minute there."

For a long moment, Arthur stared into the canvas. His breath came quicker at first, but slowly steadied, his chest rising and falling back into rhythm again. Each blink seemed to lift the haze from his eyes. He glanced at Wendi. "Sorry about that."

She gave him a reassuring smile, resting her hand lightly on his arm. "It's okay, Arthur. We're here."

Max padded over and nudged his head under Arthur's palm.

Wendi's eyes drifted from the canvas to Miles. Her unspoken question was clear.

Do I want to say it out loud?

The silence stretched out longer than it should have, becoming its own kind of answer.

Miles opened his mouth, then closed it again. He could change the subject ...

Wendi's eyes stayed on his, not pushing, just waiting—a kind of patience that somehow made it harder to look away than if she'd asked directly.

His throat tightened, and he forced the words out. "The house fire I told you about ... Mom got me out through a window." Miles swallowed hard. "The ceiling collapsed right after. She never made it out. Dad was at work when it happened."

"Miles, I'm so, so sorry." Wendi reached for his hand and closed her fingers around his.

"That's why I became a firefighter," he continued. "Thought I could save someone else's mom, I guess ... until I froze up at that warehouse fire."

The words sank into the space between them.

Miles had never voiced it like that before. He hadn't meant to say it like that—hadn't meant to say it at all. But there it was, out in the open, and somehow it felt ... freeing. He found it strange how the right words had always remained hidden behind the safe ones.

Over the years, the past had a way of convincing him he'd lost everything, that he was merely going through the motions of living while carrying the weight of what could never be changed. But something about Wendi—her quiet understanding, the warmth in her eyes that asked for nothing yet offered everything—made him dare to believe in tomorrows again.

"This isn't right." Arthur frowned at his half-finished painting. "There aren't any houses at the cove."

"It's okay, Dad," Miles said, pushing himself to his feet. "Want me to set up a fresh canvas?"

Arthur shook his head. "No. I need to save my energy for the special painting." He cleaned his brush. "That one matters most. Has to be ready by tomorrow."

Clouds rolled in from the horizon and the first raindrops splattered onto them as they packed up the supplies. Arthur insisted on wrapping his flame-painted canvas. "Part of the story," he said with unexpected clarity.

When they loaded the truck, Max stayed close to Arthur, nuzzling against him as if sensing his unease.

Before climbing into the passenger seat, Arthur paused, turning for a last look at the cove. His gazed lingered. Then he turned to Wendi and Miles. "This place remembers everything," he said softly. "Even when we forget."

13

Wendi

Wednesday

THE SCENT OF LEMON polish filled the air as Wendi adjusted the framed pastel for the fifth time, stepping back to squint at it.

Crooked. Again.

She exhaled, nudged it a fraction to the left, and stepped back.

Better.

She glanced at the wall clock. Two hours from now, she'd know if The Painted Shell had a future.

As she moved to a collection of hand-carved wooden fig-urines donated by a local artist, her phone buzzed. Another message from Laurel. The third today.

Laurel: *Have you decided yet?*

The old Wendi wouldn't have hesitated—she'd have already texted her back with a "yes" and started packing. Instead, she stuffed the phone back into her pocket. New York could wait.

Max pawed at one of the displays, dangerously close to a ceramic vase.

"Max, bed." She tapped her leg.

He hit her with the look—the one that usually got him out of trouble—then made a break for the watercolor palettes.

Too late. He crashed into the table, and the palettes clattered to the floor.

"Max!" She dropped to her knees, gathering them up. "Unbelievable."

The dog licked her cheek, clearly thinking he'd been helpful. As she returned the last palette, her stomach twisted.

What if no one comes? What am I even doing?

The bell above the door chimed. Miles stepped inside. "Fear not. The cavalry is here!"

Wendi smiled at his dad joke. "Okay, General Custer. You're early."

"Ouch. That didn't end well for him."

She smirked. "Fine. Julius Caesar?"

"Eh, that might be worse."

"General Washington?"

"That's definitely better." He nodded, glancing around the transformed space. "This looks great."

"It's getting there." She tucked a loose strand of hair behind her ear. "I was about to move those tables."

Miles waved her off, rolling up his sleeves. "I've got it." He hoisted the first table effortlessly and carried it where she pointed.

Side by side, they arranged chairs in rows facing the podium she'd borrowed from the library. Their hands brushed as they reached for the same chair. That spark again—that thing that happened every time they touched.

Not now. Focus, Wendi.

The bell chimed again. Arthur shuffled in, clutching a canvas covered with a sheet. "Hope I'm not interrupting." Arthur's eyes twinkled. "Brought something special."

Wendi stepped away from Miles, feeling heat in her cheeks. "Perfect timing. Here, let me—"

"Ah-ah," Arthur said, hugging the canvas close. "This stays under wraps till auction time. A surprise, you understand."

"Of course." Wendi nodded. "We'll save it for last." She struck a pose, hand over heart, and mouthed a lyric from "Save the Best for Last."

Arthur's bushy eyebrows knotted. "What are you doing?"

"Vanessa Williams? 'Save the Best for Last?' 1992?" His blank stare didn't budge. She gasped and clutched her chest, staggering back. "Tragic. Absolutely tragic."

Arthur shook his head. "Kids today and their music. Now, Patti Page—that was a voice. 'The Tennessee Waltz' could break your heart."

Miles chuckled, and something in Wendi's chest loosened at the sound.

Just as Arthur set his covered painting on the easel, the lights flickered. Once, twice, then again.

"Of all nights." Wendi pressed her fingers to her temple.

"You've got to be kidding me right now."

"Where's your fuse box?" Miles asked.

"Storage." She gestured toward it. "But I wouldn't know what I'm looking at."

"Let me check." Miles headed to the back, and Max trotted after him.

"Nope. Not this time." Wendi caught his collar. "Let Miles work."

The dog whined, straining toward the back-room doorway Miles had disappeared through.

Arthur chuckled, easing himself into a chair. "Guess someone's got a new favorite."

Wendi looked downward. "Et tu, Max? Thought Arthur was your favorite?"

"Ah, I'm not worried. Little guy still loves me, I'm sure."

As Arthur reached down and patted Max, she paced the length of the shop, checking her phone.

Still no new RSVPs.

The names on her RSVP list weren't exactly promising: Marjorie from the Chamber of Commerce. A couple of council members who'd said they'd "try to stop by." Mrs. Finch, whose "confirmation" was a rambling text about her granddaughter maybe coming.

Wendi sighed, scrolling through the sparse responses again. RSVPs were one thing; showing up was another thing entirely. She'd learned that lesson the hard way after the holiday craft fair, when half the vendors who'd confirmed never showed, leaving her with an embarrassingly empty shop and too much mulled cider.

The lights flickered again. Her pulse spiked. If the power

went out mid-auction ... game over.

Might as well text Laurel now.

At last, Miles emerged from the back.

"Well?" She winced at her own tone.

"We're good for tonight, but you'll need an electrician to stop by first thing tomorrow." He wiped his hands on a rag. "The wiring's BC-era old."

"Fantastic. Just what I needed." She exhaled, then softened. "Really. Thanks, Miles."

"You know I've got you. Everything else all set?"

They did a final walkthrough, adjusting displays and double-checking the bid sheets. Arthur's mystery painting stood front and center, sure to draw attention.

"I think we're good." Wendi glared at Max, who had tangled himself in ribbon.

Almost good.

"Come on, troublemaker." She scooped up Max's things, shaking her head. He followed her to her office, tail between his legs.

"You know why you can't be out there tonight, right?" She lined up his food, water, and a mangled blue chew toy. "Let's review your rap sheet, shall we? Mrs. Peterson's stolen biscuit. Councilman Baker's coffee—RIP, his new suit." Max tilted his head. "And the craft fair? A full-blown hostage situation—three people tangled in yarn, Max. Three!"

He wagged his tail.

"And we agreed never to speak of the police chief's toupee incident." She scratched behind his ears. "This is too important for Max-imum chaos, okay?"

Wendi stared at her small dog, marveling at how a thirteen-pound Yorkipoo could create such disproportionate havoc. It was almost magical, his uncanny ability to steal the spotlight—even if for the wrong reasons. She bent down and kissed the top of his head. "I'll be back soon. Be a good boy."

As she closed the door, his whine rose behind her—relentless, guilt-inducing.

The show must go on.

Back in the main area, Wendi glanced at her phone. A new text.

Emma: *Sorry girl! Stuck at a train. Save me a seat. Be there soon!*

Wonderful.

Fifteen minutes until start time. Her mouth went dry.

"They'll show," Miles said.

Arthur nodded. "Patience, young lady."

The bell chimed, and Wendi's heart jumped—only to plummet when she saw it was just Marcy and Jim from the Gazette, notepads ready.

"Evening, Wendi." Marcy peeked around. "Are we early?"

"Nope, you're right on time." Wendi managed a smile. "Make yourselves at home."

As the reporters wandered, Wendi checked her phone again. Another text from Laurel.

Laurel: *At least think about it, Wen. You're wasting your talent down there.*

The clock dragged forward. Five minutes. Then ten.

Seriously?

She scanned the empty chairs, then the carefully curated

artwork. So much work. So much hope. And still, just the five of them.

Marcy and Jim shared a look. Wendi could practically see tomorrow's headlines: *LOCAL ART SHOP'S LAST GASP FALLS FLAT or SAVE THE SHELL FUNDRAISER: NO-SHOW DISASTER.*

Where's everyone at?

"Wendi?" Marcy's voice sounded far away. "Should we wait a little longer?"

The walls pressed in.

A familiar prickle crawled up her arms.

Her breaths grew erratic, shallow, fast.

Paintings blurred, edges smearing together.

She clung to the edge of the table.

Not now. Not tonight. Please.

Laurel's text flashed in her mind: *You're wasting your talent down there.*

Footsteps approached. The scent of bay rum and cedar. "Wendi?"

14

Miles

MILES GENTLY CAUGHT HER arms. "Wendi."

No response. Her breaths came out in shallow gasps.

Miles knew panic—had hauled people from smoke-filled rooms, steadied rookies on their first bad call, and faced himself in the mirror after nights he'd rather have forgotten.

He guided her into a chair and kneeled beside her. His palm pressed lightly between her shoulder blades, feeling each rapid rise and fall of her breath. "You're okay. Breathe with me. In through your nose ..." he whispered. "Out through your mouth."

Slowly, her breaths steadied. Her gaze lifted, meeting his—embarrassment flickering beneath gratitude. "I—" Her voice trembled, and she shook her head. "I thought I'd be alone ..."

Miles traced soothing circles around her back. "Give it a little more time."

A faint smile touched her lips—it wasn't much, but it was something.

The door suddenly burst open, the bell clanging above it. Miles glanced up.

More footsteps. More voices.

The bell rang again. Then again.

Even more faces. Some familiar.

What's happening?

A woman with auburn hair rushed to Wendi's side. "Sorry we're late!"

People streamed in behind her.

Auburn-hair squeezed Wendi's hand. "Lisa was locking up when I called. Kara was feeding the animals. But when I said it was for you and the Shell—you know how they are. Katie posted on her bookshop's Facebook, and, well—" She gestured at the packed room.

Miles stepped back, observing Wendi's shoulders loosen, and the strain around her eyes fade. In its place—something softer, something that looked a lot like hope.

The woman with auburn hair turned to him and stuck out her hand. "Emma." Her smile was genuine. "Thanks for being here for her."

"Miles." He shook her hand.

Old Pete limped in with Mrs. Winters on his heels. Ada set up a makeshift bar in the corner. Phil flashed Miles a thumbs-up from his food truck window.

"Never a doubt," Old Pete said to Wendi, thunking a gallon of tea onto the table. "This town can't lose The Painted Shell."

Arthur walked up and greeted his neighbor, Mrs. Winters. "Cindy? Didn't expect to see you here tonight. Thought you'd be home with a book and that old cat of yours."

Mrs. Winters huffed. "Oh, please. When I heard what was happening, I figured someone had to make sure you weren't getting into trouble."

"Trouble?" Arthur smirked. "You always said I should put my work out there more."

"And look at you now," she said, nudging his arm. "Had me worried the other night, you know. But you look like yourself again."

Arthur gave a small nod. "Feels good to be part of something again."

No blank stares. No half-finished sentences.

Miles sighed. *Dad seems okay.*

Wendi stepped up to the podium, dabbing at her eyes. "Thank you all for being here," she said. "The Painted Shell isn't just a store or some gallery; it's home. And standing here tonight, I'm reminded of exactly why."

"Save the Shell!" someone shouted.

The chant rippled through the building.

Miles leaned against the wall, arms folded. This wasn't his town. But seeing them rally around Wendi like this, feeling the shift in the room—it unraveled something inside him.

He watched her soak it all in—her shoulders lighter, her smile brighter. He wanted this for her—more than he'd wanted anything in a long time.

Arthur, standing near the front, let out a hearty cheer.

Miles glanced at him, then moved forward and raised his voice. "Save the Shell!"

And just like that, he was part of it.

The auction kicked off—ceramic bowls, carved figures, and paintings. People bid more than they should've and paid more than what made sense.

"And now," Wendi said, "paintings by our very own Arthur Dalton."

She unveiled the first one: the cove at dawn. The sky was layered with oranges and pinks that exuded the feeling of early morning. Wisps of lavender clouds hovered above and, in the distance, a single seagull soared, while the dark silhouette of the rocky outcroppings framed the scene.

Miles tensed as the bidding started.

His dad's paintings were good—*really* good—but auction-worthy good?

"Two hundred," a voice called out.

"Two-fifty."

"Three hundred."

With each bid, Arthur stood a little taller. When it sold for five hundred, his face shone with something brighter than the sun.

The next painting: the cove in a storm. Dark clouds swirled above churning water. Waves crashed and foamed as wind whipped across the surface. Arthur had painted it on one of his better days, telling Miles about riding out a storm as a young man.

Bidding grew more heated for this one, the storm in the cove fetching six hundred. Miles added the running total in his head.

The third painting depicted the cove at sunset. The sun was going down, turning the water purple and gold. Jagged rocks framed a lone boat bobbing toward the shore.

Sold for nine hundred.

Wild!

Then, Wendi's painting was revealed—a spiral shell with bands of cream and caramel, shimmering under the blue sky, and tilted at a slight angle, giving it a dreamlike feel. The crowd hummed in admiration.

That spiral shell looked a lot like …

No—couldn't be. There are probably thousands just like it.

The bidding started low—

"Two hundred."

"Two-fifty."

—but climbed quickly.

"One thousand."

"Fifteen hundred."

"Two thousand," someone shouted, and the room went quiet for a moment before erupting into applause.

Across the room, Wendi's eyes found his. Her smile hit him like a physical thing—relief and hope mixed together. For a moment, Miles let himself imagine being part of this place for good—standing in rooms like this not as the guy passing through, but as someone who belonged, someone who was there to stay.

"Break time," Wendi called after the seventh painting sold. "Phil's got food outside. Stretch your legs. We'll be back for our final piece—a special painting Arthur made just for tonight."

The crowd spilled outside, riding the high of the night's success. Laughter and chatter carried into the cool air as the first stars dotted the deepening blue above them. Across the street, Phil's tables filled up. String lights cast an amber glow between the buildings while the scent of sweet potato fries and salt air wafted through the night.

As Miles glanced upward, he noticed how the stars were much brighter here than in Atlanta. "Congrats, old man." He clapped his dad's shoulder. "Your paintings might be the reason this place makes it."

"The best is yet to come," Arthur said, watching people milling around, admiring their new paintings. "They remember. All of them—why this place matters."

Miles nodded, struck by how present Arthur seemed tonight.

A young woman approached with a canvas tucked under her arm. "Mr. Dalton? Your brushwork is incredible—how do you get the waves to move like that?"

Arthur lit up, launching into a story about painting the coast as a boy. Miles stepped aside as his dad spoke with the ease of someone who had never forgotten his craft.

Nearby, the couple from the hardware store waved him over. "Miles! Your dad says you know a thing or two about refinishing floors?"

Of course he did.

"Just enough to be dangerous." Miles smiled and walked over. He chatted about sandpaper grits and polyurethane, nodding along to their renovation woes, but his eyes couldn't help but drift through the crowd, looking for a familiar face.

Where is she?

He excused himself after a few minutes, grabbing a paper cup of water from a table. He gulped it down and scanned the clusters of people, looking for that unmistakable red hair—for the woman he adored.

"Fire!" The primal scream sliced through the night.

Miles turned toward it.

Smoke billowed from a window at the back.

Orange flames crawled up the walls, distorted through the warping glass.

Someone yelled about 9-1-1.

He smelled it now—the nauseating sting of burning paint and canvas.

Wood splintered. Something snapped.

Miles's eyes watered as he surveyed the scene, mentally calculating.

Rate of spread: Rapid. Old wood and art supplies feeding the flames—perfect storm for engulfment.

Wind direction: East—pushing smoke and heat toward the back.

Points of failure: Cracking ceiling joists, weakening floors, and heat-stressed windows. Could explode into lethal glass shards.

"No—no, no, no!" Arthur's voice cracked, yanking Miles back from his thoughts. Tears filled his dad's eyes. "My special painting!"

"Dad, I'm sorry, but you have to get back, okay?" Miles tried to reassure him, his feet already carrying him toward the building.

He shoved through the crowd, fighting against the flow of bodies. Snatches of conversation reached him—someone said how old and dry the building was, how fast it would burn, another said the fire department was ten minutes out.

Ten minutes?

In ten minutes, there'd be nothing left.

Smoke thickened, curling through the air. Glass cracked. People shouted conflicting things—someone called for water, another yelled about an extinguisher, but Miles already knew the truth: None of that would be enough.

There she is.

Miles sprinted in Wendi's direction.

"Let me go!" she screamed, straining against the men holding her back. "My boy's in there!"

The men tightened their grip. "The fire department's coming. You can't go in there."

Flames swallowed the doorway.

Wendi's sob cut through the chaos. "Max! Please, someone—"

A blast of heat seared against his face.

Someone shouted his name—maybe his dad, maybe Wendi.

He turned. Bolted.

A hand clamped onto his arm. But nothing—not logic, not fear, not the weight of every risk he knew too well—could stop him.

He tore free. He knew exactly what this was. The kind of choice that ended careers. Or lives.

Didn't matter.

Didn't think.

Didn't stop.

And charged straight into the fire.

15

Wendi

Wendi couldn't breathe. The crowd pressed in around her, but all she saw was the burning doorway of The Painted Shell. Emma and Phil's hands gripped her arms, holding her back.

"You can't go in there," Emma said, her grip tightening.

Wendi barely heard her. Her eyes stayed fixed on the flames, willing Miles to reappear. The sirens in the distance meant nothing—they were too far away, too late.

Her mouth went dry. Her pulse thundered in her ears. Her hands shook until she clenched them into fists to stop the tremors. This wasn't like her panic attack earlier; this was different—more terrifying. Miles and Max were trapped inside.

Seconds felt like hours.

She looked skyward and whispered, as if pleading with the universe. "Please, don't take them from me."

The air split with a deafening boom. Part of the roof

collapsed, sending sparks into the night. A horrified wail ripped through the onlookers. Someone else grabbed at her, trying to pull her back.

Wendi wrenched free, pushing forward with a desperate urgency. She had to be closer for when Miles stepped out—if he made it out at all.

"He'll make it." Arthur appeared beside her. "My boy's a strong one."

The fire roared hotter. Glass shattered inside. A beam crashed down, the sound reverberating through the ground.

Around her, the townspeople coped in different ways. Ada's lips moved in a silent prayer. Mrs. Winters sobbed uncontrollably. Old Pete took off his hat and held it against his chest.

A ripple moved through the crowd.

Someone pointed.

Wendi squinted through tears. Then, for just a moment, the smoke parted, and a shape appeared in the doorway—a shadow.

Her heart nearly stopped.

"Miles!"

Without thinking, Wendi broke free and ran.

He staggered into view, bent low, cradling something to his chest. His face and clothes were coated in soot. He couldn't stop coughing.

At first, she couldn't tell what he was carrying. Then a bark. Max's head appeared, nose twitching as he emerged from Miles's arms.

Miles clutched something else flat against his side. Just as he cleared the doorway, the awning gave way, collapsing in a shower of embers.

She collided with Miles in a desperate embrace, sobs wracking her throat. Max squirmed between them, whimpering softly.

"You're okay." Her hands moved over him—his soot-smeared cheeks, his shoulders—"You're both okay."

Max licked at their faces. Miles tried to speak, but the effort only triggered another fit of coughing. His arms were marred with burns, his eyes red and bloodshot.

Wendi draped an arm around him and guided him across the street, away from the fire. He felt hot through his shirt and leaned heavily against her.

Arthur squeezed by the onlookers. "My boy," he said. "Always the brave one."

Miles straightened, holding out the covered canvas he'd protected. The sheet was singed. "Couldn't leave this behind."

Arthur took the painting, his hands trembling as he removed the sheet. The crowd gathered, momentarily forgetting the fire.

It was a painting of the cove, but unlike his others, this one had people in it ...

A small boy held a spiral shell to his ear. A red-haired girl sat nearby. A man stood at the water's edge, watching them.

"Been trying to get this one right for months," Arthur said. "Couldn't remember everything, but knew it mattered."

Wendi gasped as the memory hit her—a day at the cove

as a child, a sad-eyed boy, his distracted father.

Miles reached into his pocket and pulled out the familiar spiral shell.

"It was you," Wendi whispered, breathless with the realization.

"You?" Miles's eyes widened, turning the shell in his hand. "This got me through everything. That little girl at the cove told me it was magic."

Wendi touched the shell and their fingers brushed. "I never knew if it helped."

"Every day." Miles looked right at her. "That kindness. Your smile. I've thought about you—every single day."

"You did?"

They stood amidst the chaos—fire, sirens, and shouting voices—but Wendi only saw Miles. His hand gently cupped her face. "I think I've been looking for you my whole life."

A sharp breath hitched in her throat, but before she could speak, his lips found hers.

The world blurred.

The crackling fire, the frantic voices—they all faded. There was only Miles. He tasted of salt and smoke and something unmistakably him. The scrape of his unshaven jaw sent shivers to her bones.

She sank into him, fingers threading into his hair, pulling him closer. It wasn't just their first kiss—it was every kiss they should've had, every longing glance, every moment that had led them here. It was the feeling of coming home to something she hadn't even known she was missing.

When they finally pulled away, his forehead rested against hers. Right now, nothing else mattered.

Only this. Only them.

Max barked and circled their feet. Some people cheered. Others wiped tears away.

The fire trucks arrived, their red lights flashing across the scene. Firefighters rushed past with hoses, but Wendi knew The Painted Shell was beyond saving.

The sirens blared. The crowd murmured in low voices. The fire hissed as water hit it.

She watched them work, leaning against Miles with his arm around her. "Everything I built ..." she started, but her words faltered. "Just lost everything."

"Not everything." Miles gently turned her toward him, still holding the shell. "We'll figure it out," he said. "Together."

Wendi looked at Miles, at the honesty in his eyes, then at Max pressed against her leg, then at Arthur standing nearby.

The building burned behind them. But the panic she expected never came. Instead, she felt a quiet sadness, tempered by the warmth of Miles beside her. As his fingers intertwined with hers, Wendi realized—the shell in his hand had truly been magic after all. It had carried the sound of the cove to him until he found his way back to this place—back to her.

She squeezed his hand, feeling the lucky charm nestled between their palms.

Some things were lost, but others—more important things—were found.

Epilogue

One Year Later

Sunlight glowed against the vibrant sign of The Painted Shell as Wendi stood at the door, key in hand. The shop looked nothing like before—sleek modern lines with touches of beach charm, the building now popping with blues and oranges. After the investigators had confirmed the electrical fault that caused the fire and the insurance claim was processed, rebuilding had become possible. Alongside the insurance money, the auction had surely helped; but it was also because of the community's response. After the fire, the townspeople had organized additional fundraisers—bake sales, benefit concerts at the town square, and an art walk—all under the banner *Save The Shell 2.0*. These efforts had brought in a steady stream of donations, while volunteers showed up daily with tools and willing hands, ensuring that somehow, from ashes, something even better had emerged.

Heart swelling, she eased the door open. Inside, the transformation was even more striking. Light poured through the skylights and gone were the cramped corners and outdated fixtures. In their place: open, airy space, honey-toned hardwood floors, and handcrafted shelves. While the shop had a fresh new look, Wendi had made sure to preserve elements of its original character—the painted color wheel remained, though now mounted in a custom frame, and she'd recreated the spiral shell logo with subtle enhancements that spoke to both the past and future of The Painted Shell.

When she closed the door behind her, Max zipped around her ankles before flopping down in his usual sunny spot by the window. Her gaze landed on Arthur's framed painting on the back wall—miraculously rescued from the fire when Miles had risked everything. Young Wendi and Miles at the cove, spiral shell between them, with those words along the bottom: *It's magic. From the ocean. It'll help.*

The bell chimed. Miles walked in with damp hair, wearing his faded Hadley Cove Fire Department shirt.

"How'd the morning shift go?" Wendi asked.

"Just breaking in the rookies." Miles stretched, rolling his shoulder, revealing a scar on his arm—permanent proof of that night he'd run into the burning shop. The burns had healed but left their mark, joining that older scar Wendi always traced. He caught her staring and smiled.

"Ada's cookie day at the station." He pulled out a slightly squashed snickerdoodle. "Saved you the good one."

Wendi took it and broke off a piece. "These are good, but her chocolate chip ones are better."

"No way. Not even close." Miles slid behind the counter and wrapped his arms around her. "Aren't we supposed to be grateful for what we get?"

"That so?" She leaned into him, soaking in the moment.

The bell jangled again. Arthur walked in with his art supplies, and Max bolted from his cushion to greet him. "Bad timing?" Arthur asked, dropping his bag.

"Perfect timing." Wendi stepped back. "Your students should be here any minute."

"Great." Arthur laid out brushes on the table. His senior art therapy class had become the shop's hottest ticket. "Got something different planned for today."

Wendi watched him set up with methodical care. The good days far outnumbered the bad ones now. Under Dr. Mendez's adjusted treatment plan and the structure that came with teaching regular art classes, Arthur was experiencing longer periods of clarity and purpose.

"Need a hand?" Miles asked his dad.

"I'm good." Arthur nodded toward the corner. "Though you could get those easels lined up for me."

While Miles arranged easels, Wendi filled cups of water and set out palettes. The routine felt right, the three of them moving around each other like they'd been doing it forever.

Arthur began sorting reference photos, then glanced toward Wendi. "Mrs. Winters coming?"

"Yeah. Called earlier. Says she's dragging her new friend along."

Arthur laughed, shaking his head. "Woman never stops matchmaking."

"Never," Miles said. "Remember when she tried to set you

up with that librarian's daughter?"

"She told me my haircut made me look like a depressed porcupine." Arthur smoothed down his now-neat silver hair. "Woman doesn't hold back."

The door swung open and Emma walked in with a basket. "Delivery!" She set it down and revealed fresh-baked scones. "Thought your class might need these."

"You're a lifesaver." Wendi hugged her. "How's Barking Orders?"

"Busy, but in a good way. Had to hire two more people." Emma swept her gaze over the room. "This place is looking incredible."

"Couldn't have done it without you all." Wendi squeezed Emma's hand.

Max barked as Arthur's students filed in—mostly seniors, plus some younger folks sent by their doctors to help with stress and anxiety. They greeted Arthur like an old friend, settling at their easels with comfortable familiarity.

Mrs. Winters made her grand entrance last. "Arthur Dalton! You better have saved my spot." She breezed past him to the easel by the window. "Light's best over here."

"Wouldn't dream of giving it away," Arthur said, their back-and-forth making everyone chuckle.

As Arthur started his demonstration, Wendi checked the register and opened her ledger. The numbers told a completely different story than it had a year ago. The local paper's feature on Miles saving Max and then Arthur's painting from the fire had unexpectedly put Hadley Cove on the map for art enthusiasts from neighboring towns. Every class now had a full waiting list, and the gallery section showcasing local artists—Arthur's work included—could barely keep up. The Painted Shell had become a Coastal Georgia must-visit art destination.

Her phone lit up with a text from her old boss.

Laurel: *The new hire didn't work out. Still have a desk with your name on it. Just say when.*

Wendi looked up at her bustling shop—Arthur gesturing enthusiastically while explaining brush techniques, students leaning in, Miles organizing supplies and chatting with Mrs. Winters.

This was home.

Wendi: *Thanks, but I'm right where I belong.*

The fire had changed everything—not just the building, but her. In those first chaotic weeks, the community center had become their makeshift studio. Miles had stayed up all night painting *The Painted Shell Pop-Up* sign, complete with a spiral shell. When he hung it up, Wendi had felt it—that unmistakable shift. She was truly falling in love with him.

Through insurance headaches and endless permits, they found ways to make the hard days lighter. She still smiled thinking about their impromptu trip to Tybee Island—Miles daring her to a sandcastle competition and Max "remodeling" their creations by digging holes through the center. They'd ended the day with ice cream at sunset.

And then there was the disaster of a cooking date at Wendi's cottage. He'd been so sure she'd love making home-made pasta—something about the hands-on creativity of it seemed right up her alley. Wendi, thinking he was excited about it, had gone along with the plan, smiling through the flour dust and sticky dough. It only took fifteen minutes for them to realize they both hated it. They had stared at each other for a beat before bursting into laughter. Abandoning the mess, they grabbed sandwiches and took them to the cove instead. Sitting shoulder to shoulder, they talked until the stars came out.

Rebuilding the shop became its own kind of love story. Choosing fixtures, picking paint colors, tweaking the layout—every decision, every compromise, brought them closer. When she panicked over costs, Miles reminded her of the growing class waitlist. When he worried about overstepping, she found small ways to show him—this wasn't just her dream anymore. It was theirs.

Two years ago, she hadn't just come back to this town—she had come back to herself. And for the first time in a long while, that felt like enough. She set down her phone, the decision feeling right in a way it never had before the fire. Her eyes caught Miles's across the room. He grinned and made his way over to her.

"Think we could close early? Something's happening in town."

Wendi frowned, checking her calendar. "Nothing's scheduled?"

Emma, helping a student find the perfect red, suddenly became fascinated with a display of paintbrushes.

"Max needs his dinner," Arthur announced, far too casually for someone who never missed a lesson. "Wendi, why don't you take over?"

Max's ears twitched at his name, his tail thumping once. If dogs could smirk, Wendi was certain hers just had. She narrowed her eyes. "What are you up to?"

Arthur exchanged a glance with Miles and Emma before shrugging. "Nothing. Just thought we could use a break."

After locking up a couple hours later, Miles waited with keys in hand.

Wendi swatted his arm. "Seriously, what's going on?"

"You'll see."

"Miles ..."

"Trust me?" He pressed a blindfold into her palm.

"Always. But can you at least give me a hint?"

"Then it wouldn't be a surprise now, would it?"

With an overly dramatic sigh, she looped the blindfold into place and let him lead her away. Soon, the hum of the town gave way to the sound of steady crashing waves and the salt air grew stronger.

"You're taking me to the cove, aren't you?"

He squeezed her hand. "Maybe."

She heard whispers and the shuffle of feet. When Miles finally removed the blindfold, Wendi gasped.

The entire town had formed a human tunnel on Main Street. Old Pete, Ada, Phil, the Hendersons—faces from every part of their lives—stood in two rows, making a path straight to the beach. In their hands, they carried pieces of Hadley Cove—shells, art work, flickering candles.

"Miles ..." she whispered. "What is this?"

"You'll see." He nudged her on.

As they walked through the human corridor, familiar faces greeted them—some with tears, others with knowing smiles. With each step, more people joined behind them.

At the cove, Wendi pressed a trembling hand to her lips. The area glowed with string lights between dunes, flowers arranged in the sand, and paintings of their story displayed on easels. Arthur stood at the water's edge, Max beside him with a ridiculously large bowtie fastened to his collar. Emma, Mrs. Winters, and their closest friends formed a half-circle.

Miles faced her and took both her hands. "Wendi Parker." His voice was quiet but steady. "When I was ten, you gave me a shell on this beach and said it was magic. You were right." He reached into his pocket. "That day changed everything. I spent years trying to become someone worthy of that kindness, never knowing if I'd get to see you again."

Max trotted over with something glinting on his collar. Miles reached down and took it off. In his hand was a ring nestled inside the spiral shell they'd treasured. "It took thirty-six years, a fire, and one nosy dog, but we're here again, on the very spot we met." He kneeled, looking up at her with glistening eyes. "I don't want to waste another minute. Will you make me the luckiest man alive and marry me?"

Tears spilled over as she nodded, unable to contain the joy surging through her and into her bones. Her knees went weak. "Yes. Yes!"

The crowd erupted in cheers as Miles slipped the ring onto her finger. "I love you, Wendi." He cupped her face, his thumb brushing away a tear.

A soft, shaky laugh escaped her. "I love you too, Miles."

And then he kissed her.

It wasn't rushed, nor hesitant—it was deep, certain, a kiss that made the years apart feel like nothing more than a prelude to this moment, to this stretch of sand, to each other. His lips were warm, lingering, in a way that made her believe he wanted to memorize the shape of her mouth and the way she fit against him. Salt clung to their skin and the scent of the ocean wrapped around them.

Above, the sky blazed in streaks of rose and lavender, melting into the golden panorama. The waves mirrored the day's farewell, rippling with bands of liquid amber as they rolled toward the shore.

As the last sliver of sun dipped beneath the water, Wendi and Miles stood close, their foreheads touching, the shell resting between their hands—just like it had all those years ago.

Miles brushed a strand of hair from her cheek. "Since the day we left this cove, Wendi, we were always finding our way back."

❦

I hope you enjoyed the story, but your stay in Hadley Cove doesn't have to end today ...

Read Amelia's story next!

One summer wrote their story, but decades later, will it bring them back into each other's arms?

As eight-year-olds, Liam Wright and Amelia Jensen formed an unlikely friendship in the summer of 1948. Despite the vast difference in their social statuses, their bond deepened when they rescued a dog and named him Chip. Just when it felt like nothing could come between them, a twist of fate tears them apart.

Years later, their paths cross again. Amelia, now engaged to the wealthy Ferdinand Livingston, can't shake off the memories of the boy who had once held her heart.

With their worlds now so different, can the pull of the past bring them back to the magic of that one summer?

Get your signed copy at kerkmurray.com.

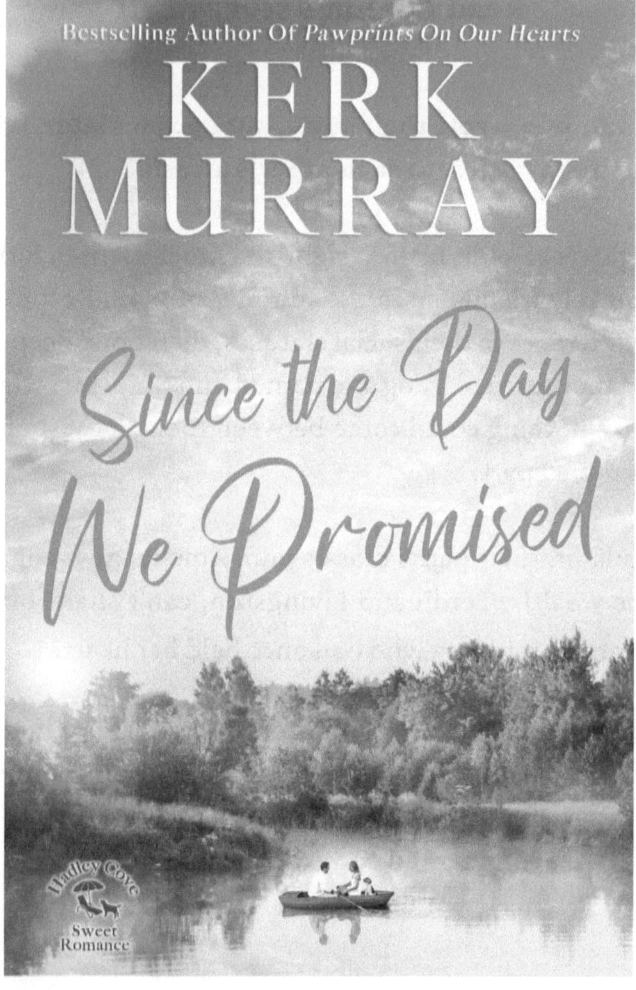
Bestselling Author Of Pawprints On Our Hearts
KERK
MURRAY
Since the Day
We Promised
Hadley Cove
Sweet Romance

Love this book? Don't forget to leave a review!

Help others discover the *Hadley Cove Sweet Romance* series. Every review matters and it matters a lot. It can be as short as one phrase to a few sentences. Wherever you bought this book, you can use this link to leave an honest review on Amazon, Goodreads, Bookbub, or your favorite retailer:

kerkmurray.com/products/reviewsincethedayweleft

Get signed paperbacks up to 40% Off

Bundle & Save at kerkmurray.com.

Apply this coupon at checkout for an additional 10% off: **GET10**

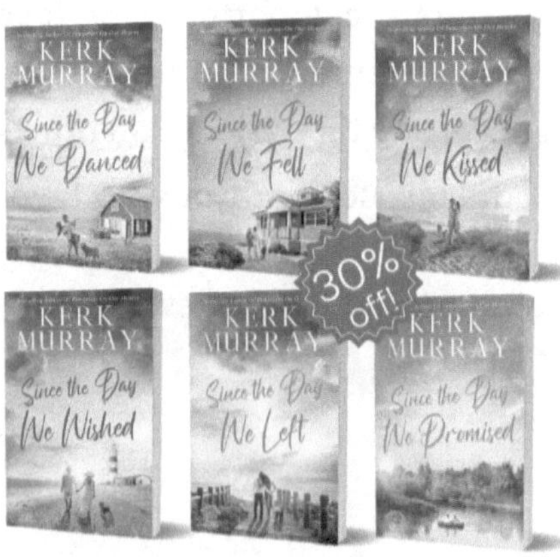

Hadley Cove Recipes

All recipes are vegan-friendly

Phil's Pumpkin Pancakes

To awaken the soul

Ingredients:

- 1½ cups all-purpose flour

- 2 tsp baking powder

- ½ tsp baking soda

- 1 tsp ground cinnamon

- ½ tsp ground nutmeg

- ¼ tsp ground ginger

- ¼ tsp ground cloves

- ½ tsp salt

- 1 cup pumpkin puree

- 1½ cups unsweetened almond milk

- ¼ cup maple syrup

- ¼ cup neutral vegetable oil

- 1 tsp vanilla extract

- 2 tbsp ground flaxseed (mixed with 6 tbsp water, as egg replacement)

Maple Pecan Syrup Ingredients:

- 1 cup pure maple syrup

- ½ cup chopped pecans

- 2 tbsp vegan butter

- ¼ tsp cinnamon

- Pinch of sea salt

Directions:

1. Mix ground flaxseed with water in a small bowl and let sit for 5 minutes to create a gel-like egg

replacement.

2. In a large mixing bowl, whisk together flour, baking powder, baking soda, all spices, and salt.

3. In a separate bowl, combine pumpkin puree, almond milk, maple syrup, vegetable oil, vanilla extract, and prepared flax egg. Whisk until smooth.

4. Pour wet ingredients into dry ingredients, gently folding together until just combined. Do not overmix. Let batter rest for 5 minutes.

5. For the syrup, combine maple syrup, vegan butter, and cinnamon in a small saucepan over medium-low heat.

6. Stir syrup constantly until butter melts, then add chopped pecans. Remove from heat and let sit to infuse flavors.

7. Heat a non-stick skillet or griddle over medium heat, lightly oiling the surface.

8. Pour ¼ cup of batter for each pancake, cooking until bubbles form on the surface (2-3 minutes).

9. Flip pancakes and cook the other side until golden brown (1-2 minutes).

10. Stack pancakes on a plate and drizzle with warm Maple Pecan Syrup.

11. Optional: Garnish with additional chopped pecans, a dash of cinnamon, or vegan whipped cream.

Additional Tips:

1. For extra moisture, add ¼ cup of applesauce to wet ingredients.

2. Adjust batter consistency with a little more almond milk if needed.

Phil's Sweet Potato Fries

To connect with others

Ingredients:

- 3 large sweet potatoes
- 3 tbsp olive oil
- 2 tbsp cornstarch
- 1 tsp sea salt
- 1 tsp smoked paprika
- ½ tsp garlic powder
- ½ tsp ground cumin
- ¼ tsp black pepper
- Optional: Fresh chopped parsley for garnish

Dipping Sauce:

- ½ cup vegan mayonnaise
- 2 tbsp sriracha sauce
- 1 tbsp maple syrup
- 1 tsp lime juice

- Pinch of salt

Directions:

1. Preheat oven to 425°F and line two large baking sheets with parchment paper.

2. Wash sweet potatoes thoroughly and pat dry with paper towels.

3. Cut sweet potatoes into uniform, thin fries about ¼ inch thick, keeping them as consistent in size as possible.

4. Place cut fries in a large bowl and drizzle with olive oil, tossing to coat evenly.

5. Sprinkle cornstarch, salt, paprika, garlic powder, cumin, and black pepper over the fries.

6. Toss fries thoroughly to ensure even coating of oil and seasonings.

7. Spread fries in a single layer on prepared baking sheets, ensuring they are not touching or overcrowded.

8. Bake for 15 minutes, then remove and flip fries using tongs.

9. Return to oven and bake an additional 10-15 minutes until edges are crispy and golden brown.

10. While fries are baking, mix all dipping sauce ingredients in a small bowl until smooth.

11. Remove fries from oven and let cool for 5 minutes.

12. Sprinkle with fresh chopped parsley if desired.

13. Serve immediately with prepared dipping sauce.

Additional Tips:

1. Soak cut fries in cold water for 30 minutes before cooking to remove excess starch for crispier results.

2. Make sure fries are completely dry before seasoning and baking.

3. Adjust baking time based on your oven and the thickness of the fries.

Ada's Snickerdoodle Cookies

To reminisce on fond memories

Ingredients:
Cookies:

- 2½ cups all-purpose flour

- 1 tsp cream of tartar

- ½ tsp baking soda

- ¼ tsp salt

- 1 cup vegan butter, softened

- 1¼ cups granulated sugar

- ¼ cup unsweetened applesauce

- 1 tsp vanilla extract

- 2 tbsp ground flaxseed mixed with 6 tbsp water

Coating:

- ¼ cup granulated sugar

- 2 tsp ground cinnamon

Directions:

1. Prepare flax egg by mixing ground flaxseed with water and let sit for 5 minutes to thicken.

2. In a medium bowl, whisk together flour, cream of tartar, baking soda, and salt.

3. In a large mixing bowl, cream together vegan butter and sugar until light and fluffy (about 2-3 minutes).

4. Add flax egg, applesauce, and vanilla extract to butter mixture, mixing until well combined.

5. Gradually add dry ingredients to wet ingredients, mixing until a soft dough forms.

6. Cover dough and refrigerate for 30 minutes to 1 hour.

7. Preheat oven to 350°F and line two baking sheets with parchment paper.

8. In a small bowl, mix coating sugar and cinnamon.

9. Remove dough from refrigerator and roll into 1-inch balls.

10. Roll each ball in the cinnamon-sugar mixture, completely coating the surface.

11. Place cookies 2 inches apart on prepared baking
    sheets.

12. Bake for 10-12 minutes, until edges are lightly gold-
    en but centers still look soft.

13. Remove from oven and let cookies cool on baking
    sheet for 5 minutes.

14. Transfer cookies to a wire rack to cool completely.

Additional Tips:

1. For extra soft cookies, slightly underbake.

2. Ensure vegan butter is softened but not melted.

3. Chill dough to prevent spreading during baking.

Storage:

1. Store in airtight container at room temperature for
   up to 5 days.

2. Freeze unbaked cookie dough balls for up to 3
   months.

Riley's Recipe Sweet Potato & Peanut Butter Treats

To bribe your fur babies

*****Please consult with your veterinarian before making any changes to your pet's diet or feeding routine*****

Ingredients:

- 1 cup mashed sweet potato (about 1 large sweet potato)

- ½ cup natural, unsweetened peanut butter

- 1½ cups whole wheat flour (or oat flour for grain-sensitive dogs)

- 2 tbsp ground flaxseed

- ¼ cup water

- Optional: 1 tbsp nutritional yeast (for added B vitamins)

Directions:

1. Preheat oven to 350°F and line a baking sheet with parchment paper.

2. Bake or microwave sweet potato until soft, then mash thoroughly.

3. Mix ground flaxseed with water and let sit for 5 minutes to create a flax egg.

4. In a large mixing bowl, combine mashed sweet potato, peanut butter, and flax egg.

5. Gradually mix in whole wheat flour and nutritional yeast (if using) until a firm dough forms.

6. If dough is too sticky, add a little more flour; if too dry, add water a teaspoon at a time.

7. Roll out dough on a lightly floured surface to ¼-inch thickness.

8. Cut into desired shapes using cookie cutters or a knife.

9. Place treats on prepared baking sheet, spacing them slightly apart.

10. Bake for 20-25 minutes until edges are golden and treats are firm.

11. Remove from oven and let cool completely on a wire rack.

12. Store in an airtight container in the refrigerator for up to 2 weeks.

Safety Notes:

1. Use natural peanut butter with **NO xylitol**. (toxic to dogs)

2. Avoid added sugars or salt.

3. Choose organic sweet potatoes when possible.

Book Club Questions

If you'd like Kerk to attend your in-person or virtual book club, please contact info@kerkmurray.com.

1. How does the prologue set the stage for the entire story? What significance does the initial beach scene hold for the narrative's development?

2. Discuss the novel's structure, which alternates between Wendi and Miles's perspectives. How does this approach enhance the storytelling?

3. The spiral shell serves as a powerful symbol throughout the book. What does it represent to different characters, and how does its meaning evolve?

4. How do Wendi and Miles's individual struggles with personal and professional identity shape their journey?

5. Compare and contrast Wendi's experiences in

Manhattan with her life in Hadley Cove. What does each environment represent for her?

6. Arthur's character is deeply affected by Alzheimer's. How does the novel portray his experience, and what insights does it provide about memory and identity?

7. Discuss the role of Max the dog in the story. How does he function beyond being a typical pet character?

8. The novel explores the concept of "home" in multiple ways. What does home mean to different characters in the book?

9. How does the theme of healing manifest throughout the story, both literally and metaphorically?

10. Examine the role of community in the novel. How do the residents of Hadley Cove support each other?

11. Discuss the novel's treatment of second chances, both in relationships and in personal pursuits.

12. What moments in the book most powerfully illustrate the connection between Wendi and Miles?

13. How does the novel handle the characters' past traumas, particularly Miles's experience with the house fire and Wendi's panic attacks?

14. The book includes several scenes of vulnerability. Which scene did you find most emotionally impactful?

15. Analyze Wendi's struggle between her corporate career and her passion for art. What does the novel suggest about following one's dreams?

16. How does Miles's career transition from firefighting reflect broader themes of identity and purpose?

17. Discuss the significance of The Painted Shell as more than just a business for Wendi.

18. How do Wendi and Miles's relationship dynamics differ from typical romantic narratives?

19. Explore the father-son relationship between Arthur and Miles. How does Arthur's Alzheimer's affect their connection?

20. Discuss the importance of friendship in the novel, particularly through characters like Emma and the town residents.

21. How does the author use the beach and the cove as more than just a setting?

22. Discuss the novel's use of memory and how it impacts the characters' present experiences.

23. Which character did you most relate to, and why?

24. How did the novel challenge or confirm your understanding of love, healing, and second chances?

25. What does the book suggest about the relationship between personal passion and professional success?

26. How does the novel explore the concept of time and its impact on relationships?

27. Discuss the symbolism of fire in the story. How does it represent both destruction and renewal?

28. What role does art play in the characters' healing and self-discovery?

29. If you could ask the author one question about the book, what would it be?

30. How might the story have been different if Wendi and Miles had not reconnected at the cove that day?

Giving Back

> "Never underestimate the power of a small group of committed people to change the world. In fact, it is the only thing that ever has."
>
> —Margaret Mead

Kerk Murray's readers make a difference. Since the release of his memoir, *Pawprints On Our Hearts*, his generous readers have raised over $20,000 toward the care of abused animals through book proceeds as well as donations to the nonprofit he founded, *The Lexi's Legacy Foundation*. If you feel compelled to donate, you can do so right here:

donorbox.org/everydollarmatters

Here's a list of the animal rescue organizations that readers are supporting monthly through each Kerk Murray book sale:

1. 2nd Street Hooligans Rescue – California

2. Cuddly – California

3. Little Hill Sanctuary – California

4. Love Always Sanctuary – California

5. Sale Ranch Animal Sanctuary – California

6. The Shore Sanctuary – California

7. Viva Global Rescue – California

8. Road To Refuge Animal Sanctuary – Connecticut

9. The Riley Farm Sanctuary – Connecticut

10. Love Life Animal Rescue & Sanctuary – Florida

11. Live Freely Sanctuary – Florida

12. Operation Liberation – Florida

13. SAGE Sanctuary and Gardens for Education – Florida

14. Farm of the Free – Georgia

15. Humane Society Greater Savannah – Georgia

16. Society of Humane Friends of Georgia – Georgia

17. Ruby Slipper Goat Rescue – Kansas

18. Shy 38 Inc. – Kansas

19. Sowa Goat Sanctuary – Massachusetts

20. Angela's Ark – North Carolina

21. Billie's Buddies Animal Rescue – North Carolina

22. Fairytale Farm Animal Sanctuary – North Carolina

23. Blackbird Animal Refuge – New Jersey

24. Broncs and Buns Rescue and Rehab – New Jersey

25. Fawn's Fortress – New Jersey

26. Happily Ever After Farm – New Jersey

27. Goats of Anarchy – New Jersey

28. Maddie & Sven's Rescue Sanctuary – New Jersey

29. Marley Meadows Animal Sanctuary – New Jersey

30. Old Fogey Farm – New Jersey

31. Rancho Relaxo – New Jersey

32. Runaway Farm – New Jersey

33. Troll House Animal Sanctuary – New Jersey

34. Wild Lands Wild Horse Fund – New Jersey

35. Happy Compromise Farm – New York

36. Sleepy Pig Farm Animal Sanctuary – New York

37. Woodstock Farm Sanctuary – New York

38. Enchanted Farm Sanctuary – Oregon

39. Harmony Farm Sanctuary – Oregon

40. Morningside Farm Sanctuary – Oregon

41. Charlie's Army Animal Rescue – Pennsylvania

42. Happy Heart Happy Home Farm & Rescue – Pennsylvania

43. The Philly Kitty Club – Pennsylvania

44. The Misfit Farm – Texas

45. Best Friends Animal Society – Utah

46. Harmony Farm Sanctuary and Wellness Center – Vermont

47. Off The Plate Farm Animal Sanctuary – Vermont

48. Gentle Acres Animal Haven – Virginia

49. Little Buckets Farm Sanctuary – Virginia

About the Author

Kerk Murray is the international bestselling and award-winning author of *Pawprints On Our Hearts* and the *Hadley Cove Sweet Romance* series. He's a romantic at heart, with a passion for celebrating life, love, and the beautiful connections between humans and animals. His soulful stories capture the essence of opening oneself up to the possibilities that love can bring, and the magic that can unfold when we do.

If you're a fan of sweet, clean and wholesome, swoon-worthy romance stories that will leave you feeling uplifted and inspired, then his novels are a must-read.

Kerk is also the founder of *The Lexi's Legacy Foundation*, a coastal Georgia 501(c)(3) nonprofit organization committed to ending animal suffering. A portion of his books' proceeds are donated to the nonprofit and together with the support of his readers, the lives of hundreds of abused animals have been changed forever.

Join him on his mission in creating a more compassionate world for all living beings, one heartwarming story at a time.

Follow Kerk on social media and sign up for his mailing list at **kerkmurray.com** to stay updated on his latest releases and sneak peeks into his upcoming works.

amazon.com/stores/Kerk-Murray/author/B09C39NLYT

goodreads.com/author/show/21719388.Kerk_Murray

bookbub.com/profile/kerk-murray

instagram.com/kerkmurray

facebook.com/kerkwrites

tiktok.com/@kerkmurray